MENNYMS ALIVE

The MENNYMS *sequence by* Sylvia Waugh *in* Red Fox

MENNYMS ALIVE

Sylvia Waugh

RED FOX

A Red Fox Book

Published by Random House Children's Books
20 Vauxhall Bridge Road, London SW1V 2SA

A division of Random House UK Ltd
London Melbourne Sydney Auckland
Johannesburg and agencies throughout the world

Copyright © 1996 Sylvia Waugh

1 3 5 7 9 10 8 6 4 2

First published in Great Britain by
Julia MacRae 1996

Red Fox edition 1997

Printed and bound in Great Britain by
Cox & Wyman Ltd, Reading, Berkshire

Papers used by Random House UK Limited
are natural, recyclable products made from wood grown in
sustainable forests. The manufacturing processes conform to
the environmental regulations of the country of origin.

RANDOM HOUSE UK Limited Reg. No. 954009

ISBN 0 09 955781 9

CONTENTS

For my mother, Alice Richardson
and my sister, Joan Porteous

He thought he saw an Albatross
That fluttered round the lamp:
He looked again and found it was
A penny postage stamp.
"You'd best be getting home," he said,
"The nights are very damp."

Sylvie and Bruno Lewis Carroll

CHAPTER 1

Where are We?

"Mum! Dad! What's happened? Where am I? Where am I?"
The voice was high-pitched with terror.

After months in limbo, Poopie Mennym had sprung to life. His arms flayed the air in movements as yet uncontrolled. The training tower that rose in front of him crashed to the floor. Pieces of rigid plastic scattered like matches spilt from a box.

Poopie had been sitting doll-still and lifeless with his back resting against the side of the bed, his feet tucked under him out of harm's way – not interfering at all with the orange plastic tower. That was how Billy Maughan had left him after building the model assault course of which the tower was the focal point. Action Men figures were carefully arranged on it and beneath it, to appear as if on manoeuvres . . .

Poopie stared, startled, at the devastation he had caused. His yellow hair was tousled. His bright blue button eyes could almost see again, but he saw as one learning to see, focussing imperfectly and feeling terror.

The room was one he had never seen before, with walls, a door and a window that had no place in his memory. The ceiling was much higher than any of the ceilings he had ever known. Poopie stood up shakily, stumbled to

11

the door with what haste he could muster, and flung it wide open.

Outside was a narrow passage lit only by fanlight windows above each bedroom door. There was no one in sight, but someone was speaking, quite loudly.

"Magnus! Magnus! Wake up! Wake up!"

Poopie was relieved to recognise his grandmother's voice calling urgently in the room next door. He dashed in. There was Granny Tulip bending over Granpa and shaking his arm. His purple foot dangled over the side of the bed. His mittened hands were beginning frantically to clutch the air.

"What? What, what what?" he muttered.

Poopie ran to Tulip's side.

"Where are we, Granny?" he cried. "How did we get here?"

Granny Tulip looked round the room, bewildered, yes, but already gaining self-control and beginning to take a measure of the situation. The last thing she could remember was being at home in Brocklehurst Grove, huddled in one room with the rest of the family and feeling irritated, waiting for something that she knew was not going to happen. But it had! My goodness it had!

For here she was, in a different house, but surrounded by many of her own belongings. She had no idea how the change had come about. It seemed impossible. To be in one place one minute, and somewhere entirely different the next. What had happened to the time between? Who had brought them here?

It would need to be accounted for somehow. Tulip, whose cheque-books were always correct to the last penny, whose skilful knitting never had the least unevenness, was quite prepared to take on the task of finding explanations. To her way of thinking, there was no question to which the answer could not be found if one looked methodically.

"I don't know how we got here," she said, looking down at her grandson, crystal eyes glittering behind her little spectacles. "But we'll soon find out."

Her appearance was the same as ever. Her blue and white checked apron was clean and neat. Above it, the little lace collar was crisp, and her dark blue dress was one Poopie had been used to see her wearing at any time in the past forty-odd years. That was tremendously reassuring.

"Where are Mum and Dad?" said Poopie, clutching Tulip's hand as if he were an infant and not a boy of ten. Poopie had always been ten. His tenth birthday came round every Christmas.

"They'll be about here somewhere," said Tulip firmly. "As soon as Granpa's properly awake, we'll go and look for them. Unless you'd like to go on ahead yourself?"

"No," said Poopie in alarm. "I'll just wait here for you."

At that moment, Magnus sat bolt upright and settled his trembling hands firmly on the counterpane, defying them to make another wobbly move. But his white moustache quivered, betraying the emotions he was trying to hide. He looked from Tulip to Poopie. He glanced round the room, the alien room that his black button eyes had never looked upon before.

The window was long and narrow with crimson curtains trailing the floor. The high ceiling had plaster all rucked up like icing on a cake. A dark floral paper covered the walls, its petals and stems closely entwined so that the pattern showed no background colour. But the unfamiliar room was not what most distressed Magnus.

Magnus the academic, Magnus who had written screeds about battles long ago, had a sudden grasp of what had happened. They had all been dead, as he had predicted. Now they were alive again. But *where* were they? And what had happened to bring this all about? To live again, anywhere

13

on this earth, was so profoundly unexpected and, to him at least, unwelcome.

"What's she playing at?" he growled, as consciousness came in uncomfortable waves. "This is not how it was meant to be . . . This should never have happened . . ."

"Well it has," said Tulip. "So you might as well get used to the idea."

"New problems," said Magnus weakly as another wave of weariness flowed over him. He was alive. He knew he was alive. But he was very, very tired.

"Fresh opportunities," said Tulip, squeezing Poopie's hand. "We have managed before, we can manage again."

"Find the others," said Magnus with no enthusiasm. "I suppose we'll have to see what must be done."

In the living-room on the floor below, Vinetta and Joshua Mennym were coming back to life, like patients emerging dozily from an anaesthetic. As their eyes became able to see again, they looked round and tried to make sense of their new and unexpected environment. Each was seated in a large armchair facing the television set.

"That's our TV set," said Vinetta. They were the first words she had uttered in many months. She looked down at the arm of her chair.

"These are our chairs," she said. Her eyes searched the room, seeing more and more familiar pieces of furniture.

"But I have never seen this room before," she concluded. The high ceiling had an ornate rose in the centre and a deep cornice round the edge. The wall-paper was dark green, embossed with faint gilt garlands. The carpet on the floor was thin and old, its pattern long-faded.

What this all meant was impossible to know in those first waking moments, but Vinetta's immediate concern was not to look for explanations but to see whether the others were there with her, and living. She glanced round at Joshua, who nodded and then shrugged his shoulders in a manner that said, what are we to make of all this?

Vinetta then looked across to where her eldest daughter, Pilbeam, was sitting in a carver chair that had come from the dining room at Brocklehurst Grove. She too was beginning to revive. She raised one arm and placed it behind her back as if to relieve stiffness. Her head turned on her neck, causing her long black hair to move from side to side, but she was still not fully conscious of her surroundings.

Next to Pilbeam, on a matching chair, sat Appleby. The red-headed fifteen-year-old was sitting stiffly upright with one hand on each chair-arm, her legs stretched out in front of her, her feet crossed at the ankles. She was wearing jeans and a brightly-patterned shirt. She showed no sign of any movement. Vinetta saw how still she was, and sighed.

When Vinetta had last seen Appleby, she had been dressed in a pink nightdress, lying in bed at Brocklehurst Grove, her long red hair brushed down onto her shoulders. She had lain like that for two whole years, no longer a personality, just a lifeless doll. And, though differently dressed now, there was no indication that her state had changed.

She has been dead longer than the rest of us, thought Vinetta sadly. Her death was different. To expect her to live again is just too much to hope for.

On the floor in front of Vinetta, Wimpey, Poopie's twin sister, began to stir, rocking backwards and resting her shoulders against her mother's knee. Awareness came slowly as she craned round to look at her parents. The expression in her pale blue eyes was dazed and wondering. She remembered the last moments in Brocklehurst Grove. She remembered the fear she had felt. Now she was in a room she could not recognise.

"Where have I been? Where am I?" she said, after

struggling to find the question she wanted to ask. She was wearing her gingham dress and her hair was tied in bunches. Nothing about her had changed, but she felt different. Her mother looked the same – black curly hair, gentle features and speckled blue eyes. Her father looked the same, his brown hair peppered with grey, his amber lozenge eyes reserved and serious.

Joshua, ever practical, stood up and walked to the nearest window. It was nothing like the windows in Brocklehurst Grove. It was a long sash window, reaching nearly to the lofty ceiling, one of a pair on the same wall. From it, in the light of a clear evening, Joshua saw the road and the river and, far away to his left, downstream, the familiar bridges that linked Castledean and Rimstead.

"Well," he said, "it may not be much comfort, but at least we're not very far from home."

CHAPTER 2

The Search

In the room next to the living-room, Miss Quigley returned to life just as the others had done. She recognised the room as a nursery, albeit an unfamiliar one. She quickly understood that life had indeed left them all on that fateful night in Brocklehurst Grove, and that it had now returned on another day in another place. She recognised the chair she was sitting in, a fireside chair that had once been in the breakfast-room.

Other things in the room were also familiar. The playpen was the one they had always had. In it sat Baby Googles. Miss Quigley gave a sigh of relief as she saw her charge bend forward and roll the ball she had been given at Christmas – a musical toy with a carousel inside its clear plastic dome.

A good nanny needs to take stock of alarming situations almost instantly. Hortensia Quigley was not simply good. She was the best! She picked up Baby Googles from the playpen and hurried to discover what was happening. The passage outside the nursery was empty but a familiar buzz of voices came from the room next door. Hortensia walked in, glanced round, and then directed her attention towards Vinetta, ignoring everyone else.

"What has happened? Where are we now?" she asked

quite calmly, as if they were travelling on a train and she was expecting to be told the name of the next station. But before her friend and employer had time to reply, Poopie burst into the room, followed by Tulip.

"That's what we want to know," he said. "Where are we and how did we get here?"

Vinetta looked at the two new arrivals. The living room was filling up with people. But was everyone there? Was everyone safe?

"Where's Granpa?" asked Vinetta anxiously. "Is he all right?"

"He's in his own bed in the room above this one," said Tulip. She looked round the room. "But where's Soobie?" she added. "I haven't seen him."

"Soobie!" shouted Poopie, going to the doorway and looking up the stairs.

There was no answer.

Then began a search of the house. Every room was checked, every cupboard door opened. They discovered that they were in a two-storey flat, topped by attics with four little arched windows tucked under the eaves. A narrow staircase led down to ground level. Joshua went downstairs to the little lobby but all he found there was an outer door that led to the street. On the window over it, the number 39 appeared in reverse.

At the front of the flat, facing out to the street, were the living-room and the nursery. To the rear was a large, square kitchen, very basic and old-fashioned, its most prominent feature a black fire-range with a side-boiler, all set in a huge, dark chimney. Next to the kitchen was a deep cupboard, large enough perhaps to be called a stock-room, full of packing cases and carefully stacked small furniture. Adjacent to that was a small bedroom, which, Miss Quigley noted, gave easy access to the nursery.

"That will be my room," she said, accepting the present situation without question, as if this were a new game about to begin. She had spent more than forty years pretending that a hall cupboard was her own little house. She had never questioned why that should be. So it seemed quite normal that another house should become home to her. Her good, practical intelligence did not extend to asking profound questions or peering too far round the next corner. Tulip looked at her sharply, marvelling at her obtuseness, but said nothing.

On the floor above was the room where Granpa was lodged, and next to it was Poopie's tiny room, the floor completely covered in bits of training tower. The searchers looked in on Granpa, explained briefly what they were doing, and hurried out before he could delay them. It was not too difficult. Magnus was still very tired, slipping in and out of sleep, and not yet concerned to take command.

The rear rooms on this floor, one quite large, the other only slightly smaller, looked out onto a concrete backyard with high brick walls. The larger room was clearly meant for the parents – it held the bed that had come from Joshua and Vinetta's room in Brocklehurst Grove. The other room had a cluttered look – three single beds and an assortment of bedroom furniture, all recognisably culled from their old home. This was a girls' room, with girls' clothing crammed into two wardrobes and a big chest of drawers.

There was no sign of Soobie, not anywhere in the flat. There was not even a room that could conceivably be his.

Pilbeam did not join in the search for her twin. She was still too dazed. She remained in the living-room sitting by Appleby. Without thinking, she reached out to grasp her sister's hand. Her fingers closed round it and held it tight.

The others returned to the living-room, baffled and distressed at their failure to find Soobie.

Vinetta shivered at a thought that came to mind.

"We have all been brought here by someone," she said. "Someone must have thought well enough of us to want us to have this house. Could they have made a mistake about Soobie?"

"A mistake?" said Tulip. "What sort of mistake?"

Vinetta struggled to find the right words, hardly daring to say them.

"He *is* blue," she said. "Maybe . . . whoever it was . . . thought he didn't match the rest of us. They haven't brought him here. Goodness knows what they've done with him."

The thought put into words, Vinetta looked desolate. Joshua placed one hand firmly on her shoulder.

"No," he said. "That was not the way of it."

Vinetta gave him a look of surprise. What did he mean, sounding so positive?

"Then why isn't he here? Everyone else is." She looked across at the motionless figure of Appleby. Pilbeam, holding onto her sister's hand, looked back at her mother, but was still not ready, or perhaps not able, to speak.

"I think," said Joshua, speaking slowly as usual, "that they might not have found him at all."

"How could they not?" said Vinetta. "He was there in the room with the rest of us."

On the first of October, how long ago not one of them yet knew, all of the Mennyms had gathered in one room to wait for life to end. For forty-six years they had lived at Number 5 Brocklehurst Grove, sharing a life given to them by their maker, Kate Penshaw. Then Sir Magnus began to have premonitions that Kate's spirit was going to leave them. He even predicted the day and the hour.

On that fateful day, by his decree, they all gathered in the little room that had once been Appleby's but now became 'the doll-room', a sort of toy cupboard for oversized dolls.

They sat in chairs brought in for the purpose, except for Appleby who lay in the bed where she had lain for the past two years. Soobie's chair was the one nearest to the door.

"Soobie left the doll-room before the end came," said Joshua. "I saw him slip out."

"Well, where did he go?" said Vinetta.

"I think he must have gone up to the attic," said Joshua. "It's what I would have done if I'd thought about it."

They sat silent. The first wave of bewilderment had passed over. A second, more powerful and more terrible, followed as each one realised that their present condition was more full of unknowns than anything they had ever experienced in nearly half a century.

"Whoever brought us here won't just leave us," said Tulip at last. "They're bound to come back some time. Then what are we going to do?"

She was about to suggest holding a meeting in Granpa's room, as of old, when something so stupendous happened that all she could do was gasp.

CHAPTER 3

What Do I Know?

The watch on his wrist told Soobie that the time was seven-thirty in the evening and the date was the tenth of May. But what day was it? What day of the week?

He sat back in the rocking chair and gave that minor problem serious thought. And compared to everything else, the problem was miniscule.

Soobie Mennym, the blue rag doll, was life-sized and living, and from a distance looked no different from any other young man. He had been one of a large and loving family. But now he was all alone.

For forty-six years, following the death of Kate Penshaw, the woman who had spent half her life making the dolls, Soobie and the rest of the Mennyms had lived here at Number 5 Brocklehurst Grove, a house large enough to accommodate all eleven of them in comfort, and private enough for them to lead a comparatively untroubled existence. Their life began within hours of their maker's death. That they were different from everybody else in the street, in the town, in the whole wide world, was something that outsiders had never suspected. Who would imagine, in their wildest dreams, that the people who came and went in the house along the road were

22

not human beings but dolls covered in cloth and stuffed with kapok?

In all that time, they never aged. Soobie was and would always be a very mature teenager. Just one member of his family had ceased to live, and even that was not like the death of a human being. Appleby Mennym simply became inanimate, lying serene in her bed and cared for by Granny Tulip as if she were a saint in a shrine.

Then, on Tuesday the first of October, just over seven months ago, the ghost of Kate Penshaw departed, leaving a room full of lifeless dolls. Only Soobie, curious and tired of waiting, had slipped away minutes before and gone alone to the attic . . .

Those left in the room below were drained of life. Not Soobie. When the final moment came, he became immobilised but remained fully and terrifyingly conscious.

The first of October was a Tuesday, thought Soobie as he rocked slowly in the chair. *So the twenty-ninth of October would be a Tuesday.* He worked his way painstakingly through November, December . . . right up to May, checking and double-checking his arithmetic. *Saturday*, he said to himself when he finished his calculations. *Today must be Saturday.*

That problem solved, his mind was at last free to consider all the other things he knew, things that would surely be important in any effort to take up the threads of life again.

One fact was clear to him. When it came to the point, Kate Penshaw had been unable to desert her people. The other dolls had died, as they were all meant to do, himself included, but a bit of Kate's spirit had clung to Soobie, like a bur in his clothing, refusing to make the final separation. Soobie, unlike any other member of his family, was blue from head to foot, a misfit made on a whim. This perhaps was why his maker had loved him so much that she could not leave him.

He got up from the seat and walked stiffly round the attic, trying out his limbs for movement, bending his elbows, flexing his fingers. The door that led to the stairs was shut. To leave the attic, to go down into the house, was something he was not ready for, not yet. Look before you leap, as Granpa would surely say.

So Soobie sat down in the rocking-chair again and dredged up the knowledge he had acquired over the past months. In the time of his paralysis he had heard many sounds in the house, sounds telling him that the whole building, except for the forgotten attic, was being emptied of furniture and carpets. The rest of the dolls were removed from Appleby's room and put into crates. So much Soobie discovered as he strained to listen to the workmen's raised voices.

Those months were torture. Soobie lived on, but his immobility was worse than death. It was fortunate that his left arm settled across his lap. That way he was at least able to see his watch, that wonderful Christmas present his father, Joshua, had bought for him. It told the time and the date and had a battery that would last not months but years.

Yesterday, thought Soobie, that girl moved my arm.

And for twenty-four hours he could not see what time it was. For twenty-four hours, he thought he might never be able to see the time again.

He did not know the girl who came into the attic so unexpectedly. She was not alone. Her name, he learnt, was Lorna. Then, with a shock, Soobie recognised her companion. It was Albert Pond! He knew Albert well enough. Albert had once been almost a member of the family, sent by the ghost of Kate Penshaw to save them when Number 5 Brocklehurst Grove had been threatened with demolition.

Albert had no recollection of this episode in his life. Powers beyond even Kate's understanding had removed the whole sequence from his memory. Albert looked at Soobie and saw only a rag doll.

Soobie wanted desperately to speak, but it was impossible. All he could do was listen. It was clear from what passed between Albert and Lorna that, except for this attic, Number 5 Brocklehurst Grove was completely empty, ready for its new owner.

Where were the rest of the Mennyms – Granny and Granpa, Mother and Father, the brother and the sisters, and Miss Quigley, the baby's nanny? Listening carefully and using his powers of deduction, Soobie concluded that they were all being cared for by a lady called Daisy. Probably in a house somewhere on North Shore Road. And Daisy, some day soon (but no sooner than next weekend – Albert mentioned taking her the key next Saturday) would be coming to the attic, to see the blue doll and, presumably, to take him away to join the others.

After Albert and Lorna left, the agony of all those months welled up in Soobie. His whole being cried out to Kate in a wordless, savage prayer. He begged for life – or death. But 'begged' is hardly the right word. He clamoured, raged, howled, implored, demanded, refusing to be ignored. Though no word could pass his lips, his thoughts would not be silenced. And this, at last, was the answer.

But the life he begged for was not just his own. *All of us*, he said, *all of us*. So it followed that somewhere, somehow, the rest of the Mennyms must also have been restored to life. Even more terrifying for them than for me, he thought. What must they be thinking? What will they do?

It was growing dark. Soobie got up and walked to the attic door, opened it very cautiously, reached out one hand and switched on the light by the switch on the landing. The risk of anyone seeing a light in windows that were set in the roof, he decided, was not worth worrying about.

He sat down again. I *am* in an empty house, he thought, and I have at least a week to sort out what can be done. Daisy cannot come in here without a key. And Albert had said he would not be taking her the key till next weekend.

CHAPTER 4

All of Us

"Appleby!"

Pilbeam's startled shout made all the others look towards her.

The hand beneath Pilbeam's hand had moved. Now, it struggled free with an impatient movement typical of its owner.

Appleby's hands fell to her lap and she looked down at them with a puzzled expression on her face. Her lips became mobile, capable of shaping words again. Her green eyes flickered. She gazed around her, recognising immediately that she was in a location and a situation that did not make any sense. Deep inside she was terrified and totally bewildered. But not for an instant would she show her feelings!

The others continued to stare at the chair where she sat. Appleby stared back at them, impudence bubbling to the surface. Then she spoke!

"What are you all looking at me for?" she snapped. "Have I grown two heads or something?"

It was the shock they needed. It was the old abrasive Appleby. Her look forbade them to comment. But Vinetta could not stop herself from trying to clasp her daughter in her arms. Her joy at that moment blotted out the problems of their present predicament, however strange and frightening it might be.

Appleby glared up at her mother and vigorously pushed her arms away.

"Stop it!" she shouted. "I hate people making a fuss. You know I do."

"But you're alive," said Vinetta, letting her arms fall to her side. "You're alive again!"

"So what?" said Appleby. "That's no big deal. We're all alive. What's so special about being alive?"

Her green eyes glittered with fury.

Vinetta did not heed the warning. She was too filled with her own emotions to be silenced.

"But you were dead," she went on. "For two long years you lay in your bed and never stirred. I never thought to see you move, to hear you speak again."

Appleby jumped up, pushing her chair back so that it nearly tipped over. Pilbeam shot out a hand to save it.

"I don't want to hear another word," shouted Appleby, fists clenched, body rigid with rage. "You're talking rubbish. I'm no different from anybody else."

In a sense, it was true. They had all been dead. Now they were all alive again. Appleby, being longer dead, had taken longer to return to life. That was all.

"Leave her," said Tulip, recovering from the shock she had felt at seeing Appleby move again. "She hasn't improved with keeping. That's well to be seen!"

For two years Tulip had tended this granddaughter with a loving care that was almost reverent, but now that Appleby was alive again and as cheeky as ever, all that would change.

Appleby glared at her but did not speak. She looked at the unfamiliar room and gauged that something momentous must have happened. How much ignorance should she admit to? It was a problem and no mistake!

"Well . . . where are we?" she was compelled to say at last, settling once more on her chair and fixing her eyes on Pilbeam. "How did we land up in this place?"

"Not from choice," said Granny Tulip, peering at her granddaughter over the rims of her spectacles. "We don't *know* where we are, or how we got here."

"So," said Appleby slowly, "we left Brocklehurst Grove, and we found ourselves here without knowing how or when. But how long ago was that?"

No one answered.

"Well?" said Appleby looking round at all of them aggressively.

Then . . .

CRASH!

From the room above came a thud heavy enough to bring down flakes of white paint from the ceiling. Granpa Mennym, fully alert now, was fed up with being ignored. Shouts had brought no response. So he heaved himself up on his pillows, leant over the side of the bed, and deliberately tilted the bedside cabinet till it fell with a crash to the floor. A wooden bowl full of ornamental fruit fell with it and spilt its contents onto the rug.

"That's Granpa," said Tulip, not displeased at the diversion. "We have kept him waiting long enough. If ever there were an occasion for a conference, this is it."

CHAPTER 5

The Conference

Tulip went first into Magnus's room, righted the cabinet and gave a loud 'tut' in her husband's direction. Vinetta, following, picked up the fruit bowl and put the pieces of fruit back in place.

"About time you all remembered me," said Granpa, glaring at them. "Get yourselves in here and find somewhere to sit. We've got some figuring out to do. We'll have to . . ."

His voice tailed off as he saw the last arrival standing framed in the doorway. The others had come in. Appleby deliberately made a grand entrance! She was not quite sure what it was she had to brazen out, but brazen it out she would. If there was any fuss to be made, she would be the one to make it! She held one hand high against the door jamb and the other stiffly on her hip.

Magnus leant forward in his bed, the pillows behind him tumbling, his velvet mouth open in mute amazement.

Tulip looked at him sharply.

"Yes, she's here," she said, flashing a look of annoyance at her granddaughter, "and back in form as you can see. Pull yourself together, Magnus. Tell her you're pleased to see her and get it over with!"

Appleby pulled a face, and that convinced her grandfather he was not just seeing things.

"Appleby," he said, almost choking on the name. "Appleby! This . . . this is wonderful."

"Don't you start," said Appleby. "I've had enough already. I'll give you fair warning. I'm not going to stand for a lot of sentimental rot. Least said, soonest mended. That strikes me as being one of your better pearls of wisdom, Grandfather."

She went up to the bed and flopped down on the rug, resting her back against the cabinet. Granpa ignored her sarcasm. Coming from Appleby it was tolerable, even welcome! His own unexpected return to life had given him nothing but heartache, a weariness for what lay ahead, a yearning for some great unknown. But here was Appleby, his best loved grandchild, coming back into their lives and bringing with her the energy he dimly remembered from his own invented youth.

"So where do we go from here?" he said gruffly, directing his question to everyone in the room, but clearly expecting any answer to come from Appleby. In his eyes, she was the cleverest of them all. He was not disappointed.

"We must begin," said Appleby smoothly, "by pooling our knowledge and then trying to make sense of all we know." It was a brighter suggestion than any of them realised. If they pooled their knowledge, Appleby would be able to catch up on things she had missed.

"Dad says Soobie's been left behind in the attic at Brocklehurst Grove," said Poopie, his blue eyes bright under the yellow fringe. "And I know that someone has been playing with my soldiers."

Joshua gripped the pipe that was still in his hand.

"We also know where this house is," he volunteered.

The others looked at him.

"It's in North Shore Road," he said.

"North Shore Road?" said Vinetta.

"Obviously," said Joshua. "Where else would we have that view from the window – the river straight ahead, the bridges and the quayside away to our left? And the number over the front door is thirty-nine. We are now living at 39 North Shore Road."

"It's an upstairs flat," said Tulip. "What is on the ground floor?"

Her crystal eyes looked down at the faded carpet as if she were trying to see through it, and through the floorboards, to the room beneath.

"We don't know yet," said Joshua. "That is one of the first things we shall have to find out. It won't be difficult."

Wimpey, sitting on a wicker trunk in the far corner of the room, looked wonderingly at the grown-ups.

"How did we get here?" she asked quietly. "Why are we here?"

"We were brought here whilst we were not conscious," said Vinetta, pleased with herself for thinking of a nice euphemism to cover their death. "Somebody must have wanted us to be here."

"So somebody," said Appleby, "must think that we belong to them."

"We do," said Granpa sombrely. "I know that. I knew it as soon as I woke up in this confounded room. We have become somebody's property."

"No we haven't," said Tulip. "They might think we are their property, but we belong only to ourselves and to each other."

"Try telling that to our new owners when they appear," said Magnus. "See what effect it has!"

"Now we come to the point," said Appleby. "We know that whoever put us here, whoever owns this building, will be coming back. They will believe that we are inanimate rag dolls. And it is vital that they should never suspect anything else."

That gave them all pause for thought. From the very beginning, nearly half a century ago, they had avoided human contact. Only one human being had ever known them and that had been Albert Pond, a very special human being, not just some casual acquaintance who might walk in from the street. He was Kate's great-nephew, summoned to their aid by Kate herself, and then made to forget them when the crisis was over.

"We'll have to freeze as soon as anyone begins to climb the stairs," said Joshua. "That staircase at least gives us some protection. We will hear the door open and shut. We will hear footsteps on the stairs. The carpet's not very thick. That didn't come from Brocklehurst Grove!"

"If only everything were that simple!" said Tulip. "When the owner returns, he or she will expect to find us exactly where we were put. We'll probably get away with small discrepancies, but any big difference would be noticed and queried. We can't, for example, all be found in this room."

"Yes," agreed Vinetta, "before ever anyone comes up here, we must return to the positions we were in when we first awoke."

Even Miss Quigley, seated on a stool by the door, nursing Googles in her arms, was worried by now. It would take time to train Googles to freeze in the corner of the playpen, to sit absolutely still and not reach out for anything. It might even be impossible.

"It would help if we knew when all this was likely to happen," she said, looking anxiously at Vinetta.

"Not tonight, I should think," said Tulip, nodding towards the window where the light was beginning to fade.

"There's obviously no one at home on the ground floor at

the moment," said Pilbeam. "The noise we've made would have been enough to bring them up to investigate. We've made no attempt to be quiet."

Suddenly Vinetta was struck by a thought that had so far troubled no one else.

"We don't even know what day it is," she said.

"There's a way we might find out," said Appleby. "The television in the living room. If that is working, we should be able to discover something."

Vinetta stood up to go and spotted an apple she had missed earlier when restoring the fruit to the bowl.

"That's another thing we'll have to be careful of," she said. "It is not just ourselves that will have to be where we were. Nothing in the house must be too much out of place."

Poopie gasped.

"My training tower!" he said. "I knocked it over. It's the first thing I remember seeing – all the pieces flying across the floor."

Joshua, glad of a way to be useful without entering into any more long conversations, said, "Come on then, son, I'll help you to build it up again. That's something *we* can put right."

Leaving Sir Magnus propped up in his bed, with promises not to neglect him for long, the others all hurried down to the room below. Vinetta switched on the television.

"I hope it is working," she said as she pressed the buttons. Sound came through and the screen brightened. The picture was not perfect. Through the 'snow' on the screen, they all made out the familiar sight of numbered balls spinning in a transparent casing. "And the first number is . . ." said the compère's voice.

"It's the lottery," said Pilbeam, "the National Lottery. It must be Saturday."

Appleby knew nothing about the lottery. It was a gap in her

knowledge which she noted briefly as she accepted Pilbeam's deduction.

"That's all right then," she said. "If it's Saturday evening, my guess is that we'll not be troubled at all till Monday. The flat below us is likely to be some sort of shop or office. That would explain there being nobody there to hear the noises we've made."

The television picture became more blurred and the sound seemed to be failing.

"And the bonus ball is . . ." said the compère in a crackly voice, but before he could pronounce the number, the sound dried up completely.

"Some use that is!" said Tulip as she turned off the set.

CHAPTER 6

Soobie

Soobie sat in the rocking-chair. After months of involuntary stillness, there was now a *need* to be still as he tried to come to terms with what had happened, and what was likely to happen.

When the skylights in the roof above him became dense black, he got up again and walked around the attic. He crossed to the other door, the door that had once been magical, that had seemed to lead to another world in another unknown dimension. It was open wide to the wall, on rusty broken hinges. Its doorway was entirely bricked up, the bricks well-aged, the plaster old and crumbling.

Soobie ran the tips of his fingers lightly across the rough surface, wary of clicking them. So the magic has gone, he thought. This door will never again lead anywhere . . .

The Mennyms had been frightened but fascinated by the door that Appleby had been forbidden to open. She *had* opened it, just a fraction, but a fraction too much. Whatever was on the other side had begun to drain the house of life. Appleby, terrified, had fought back and had died. Then, on the night two years later when all of the Mennyms ceased to live, the door had swung gently open and a kindly light had entered the attic. Was it friend or foe? Mystery, oh mystery!

And what now? Soobie looked at the brickwork, the physical reality. That doorway had been Kate's way out, her spiritual path to whatever is beyond this earth. Now only the material existed, as if the spirit world with all its hopes and all its fears had ceased to be. *For us, that means life*, thought Soobie. *What does it mean for the woman who made us?*

Forget it, said a voice in his head, speaking firmly. Forget it, and get on with living.

It was very dark outside now. The watch told him that it was ten to eleven. So he decided that now was the time to move on. He went out of the attic, switched off the light at the doorway and cautiously began his explorations. He was totally sure that the house was empty, but he moved as quietly as he could. When the stairs creaked, he increased the weight he put on the bannister so that he could tread more lightly.

He then walked carefully along the landing of the top floor, keeping to the left, his guide to the next flight of stairs. There was nothing to light his way and he was alert for obstructions, though there were none. The bare boards beneath his feet presented no difficulty for his trainers with their strong soles. He followed the wall with his left hand, past the closed door of Miss Quigley's room.

At Granpa's door he paused, considered, then opened it and looked in. The curtains were partly open and light from the street made it possible to see just how bare the room was. Not a stick of furniture remained. The carpet was gone from the floor. Not even a picture was left on the wall. The only object in the room was the telephone, tucked up against the skirting board on the floor beneath the window.

Soobie came out and closed the door. He made his way to the ground floor without inspecting any other rooms, knowing that they would all be the same. He sat on the bottom step of the stairs, as his father had once done long ago. He cupped his chin in his hands and he pondered on what to do next.

Suddenly it became clear what he must do. He knew where the rest of the Mennyms were, or thought he did. Not the actual house, but the street – and the street might hold some clue.

I'll jog down to North Shore Road, he thought, and see what I can see. For some years now, Soobie had been used to jogging along the streets of Castledean late at night. Tonight he would do so again, but with a far more serious purpose.

He went through the kitchen to the back door and there came up against his first obstacle. The door was secured with three strong bolts and a mortice lock. Unbolting it would be no problem. But there was no way he could open that lock. He rattled the handle, but knew that his efforts were futile. He looked round the room, wondering whether to exit and enter by a window. He could not go out without considering how he would get back in.

Then he remembered the spare key. It might still be there, it might not.

The kitchen at Brocklehurst Grove was not antique, but neither was it full of modern units and fitted furniture. The only 'unit' was a cupboard under the bench next to the sink. It had a drawer and in the drawer, right at the back, there had always been a little wooden dish in which was kept a spare key for the back door.

Soobie held his breath as he opened the drawer wide, wide, wider. There at the back was the wooden dish. He lifted the lid and saw the key lying untouched. He picked it up and let himself out.

Leaving the house with the utmost caution, he moved along the outer walls and round the hedge to the front gate. He stayed close to the hedges all the way to the end of the street, though there wasn't a soul in sight.

Once clear of the Grove, he began to jog as of old,

head down and well-covered by his hood. He felt in his pockets and found that his goggles were still there. That gave him additional protection. In the darkness, he was not recognisably blue.

He jogged along the High Street, past the Market Place, and then turned off into the long broad road that curved down to the river. It was a pleasant night, quite warm for the time of year. There were a few people around at the top of the street, going about their business and paying no attention to anyone else. By the time Soobie reached the bottom of the hill, under the majestic railway viaduct, he had the whole place to himself.

It had taken him about half-an-hour to reach the riverside. Once there, he slowed down and looked around him. He was on North Shore Road, the darkest part of the river's reach. The city that never slept was half a mile downstream under the well-lit bridges. Here, on North Shore Road, the middle of the day was quiet; the middle of the night was silent as the grave. Even the street lamps were smaller and dimmer than anywhere else.

Soobie jogged along the path on the side nearest the river. This pavement, old and uneven, crudely edged a broad, modern promenade. Between the tiled promenade and the buildings on the other side of the road was a gap of centuries. These buildings had once been home to wealthy merchants who 'lived over the shop', goldsmiths, silversmiths and jewellers. Now they were mainly offices and warehouses, with one or two less exalted shops in between.

The shops were all shuttered and would remain so till Monday morning. Signs over their doors, and glimpses through wire mesh, gave some indication of their wares.

Soobie looked up at the buildings, all at least three or four storeys high, all looking dark and grim.

Where was he to start? His family was in one of those buildings — somewhere.

They might as well be on the moon, thought Soobie bitterly after he had walked the length of the street several times. They don't know I am here and I don't know how to reach them.

A solitary car came towards him. Soobie lowered his head, pulled his hood well down, crossed the street and jogged up a steep lane that led in the general direction of home. It was just round the corner from Daisy's shop, but Soobie had no way of knowing that.

CHAPTER 7

What to Do Next

Vinetta drew the curtains across both windows in the living-room. They were heavy curtains, made of thick green brocade with a lining yellowed like pages in a very old book.

"We can't sit in the dark," she said, "whatever the risk. These curtains won't let out a chink of light. And the street is empty anyway."

Everyone except Sir Magnus was in the living-room now. It was, for one reason and another, a very subdued assembly. Appleby was still acutely conscious of not quite belonging yet. Her glance flitted furtively from one to another. The anger she had felt at first was gone. Her confidence was returning and the need to bluster was over, but she was still struggling with strange ideas. Miss Quigley was quietly worrying herself frantic over how she would manage to teach Googles to be still and silent when the need arose. The rest of them were simply bewildered.

"My training tower's all right now," said Poopie, in an effort to be positive. "Dad found every single bit."

Tulip, sitting on a high-backed chair that she had set in the centre of the room so that she faced all of them, gave Poopie an impatient look which he failed to notice.

"Now," she said, "we must really get down to business. We need to consider very carefully what we are to do next."

But whenever Tulip said 'we' it invariably meant someone else, acting on her instructions. That was how it had always been. The others looked at her warily.

"Joshua," she said, turning her crystal gaze on her son, "we are very fortunate. Your outdoor coat is in your father's wardrobe. I couldn't believe our luck when I saw it! You will be able to go out."

This did not startle Joshua at all. It was no more than he expected. With or without the coat, he knew he would have to leave the flat some time. And he was well used to the streets of Castledean by night.

"Where do you want me to go?" he said. "Apart from finding out what is on the floor below us, what else would you like me to do?"

Tulip's answer was crisp and to the point.

"Walk as far as Brocklehurst Grove. Look out for any sign of Soobie. See if our old home is lived in yet."

Joshua nodded.

"And buy a newspaper if you can find a vendor anywhere at this time of night. That way we'll find out the day, the month, and, more important, the year."

"The year?" said Vinetta.

"Yes," said Tulip. "For all we know we might have slept for a century. Though I doubt it. It is my hope and belief that not even one year has passed."

"And if it has?" said Pilbeam, looking at her grandmother shrewdly, knowing that something must hinge upon this question of time. Appleby, who had lost two years before all this ever happened, or so they said, listened anxiously for the answer. Did being inanimate for more than a year do some irreparable damage? She looked furtively down at herself, clenching her fists and curling her toes inside her shoes. She didn't *feel* any different . . .

Tulip's reply set her mind at rest on that score.

"If our absence from life has lasted for more than a year and a day," she said, "we will be much poorer. In fact, we will be virtually penniless. That, if you remember my telling you, is the arrangement I made with the bank and the building societies. They all have letters to be opened after that time has elapsed, and the letters instruct them to close our accounts and give all of our money to various charities."

Her words made Joshua aware of a small difficulty. Pounds were not his immediate concern. But he would need pence.

"I am penniless now," he said. "How do you expect me to buy a newspaper?"

"No problem," said Tulip. "Virtually does not mean absolutely. There is a little ready cash at our disposal. If I may borrow one of your hairgrips, Hortensia . . ."

They all gave her a look of puzzlement. Miss Quigley was as puzzled as any of them, but she would not have had the temerity to ask why, and, besides, she always felt disarmed when Tulip called her 'Hortensia'. She handed Googles over to Vinetta and immediately removed a long, thin hairgrip from her bun.

"Will that do?" she said.

"That's fine," said Tulip, feeling the sharp end of the hairgrip. "Now I'm going to see Magnus. I won't be more than a few minutes. I'll bring your coat down for you, Joshua. There's no need for any of you to come up."

Magnus had dozed off again. This new situation was exhausting, a very bad, bewildering dream. If he must go on living, he wanted to be Sir Magnus Mennym again, lodged in his own room at Brocklehurst Grove. He wanted to be free of all these dreadful uncertainties.

"Rouse yourself, Magnus," said Tulip. "Sleeping will get us nowhere. I have work to do."

"Work?" said Magnus, coming sharply to attention. "What work?"

Tulip drew a stool up to the side of the bed.

"Rest your foot on this," she said, "and keep it still."

Magnus glared at her but did as he was told. Then he remembered. In his foot, his precious purple foot, the left one, Tulip had hidden the family fortune. It was a thought, an up thought rather than a down thought, but not 'up' enough to cure his despondency.

"Much good money will do us now," he growled. "We're stuck here. No amount of money will get us out of this mess."

Tulip said nothing. Only she knew exactly how much there was in the bank and the building societies. Only she knew how the money might some day be used. She drew the curtains and switched on the light. Then she sat down and, taking the hairgrip between finger and thumb, began carefully to unpick the stitching of a seam that ran along the edge of Magnus's foot, from the base of the heel to where his little toe would be, if he had toes.

Bits of kapok fluttered like feathers from the hole she made. Then, when the opening was wide enough, she put in her hand and drew out a brown paper parcel. It was well-sealed and tightly packed.

"Now," she said, "you must not let your foot hang over the side of the bed till I have repaired it. Keep it on the stool, or on the bed if that's more comfortable. It shouldn't be hard to find some material to stuff it with. But first I must see to this parcel."

Tulip undid the package, unrolling it across the top of the bedside table from which she first removed the bowl of fruit.

WHAT TO DO NEXT

The parcel lay in a straight line with a variety of things in pouches, a bit like a toolkit. Only these pouches held bank books, credit cards and a bank card that could give access to money from the cash machine. Of more importance at the moment, however, was the small purse that contained coins of various denominations and a couple of five pound notes.

"That will do," said Tulip removing some of the cash. Then, on a thought, she also picked up the bank card. "I'm just popping downstairs, Magnus. I won't be long."

Magnus looked at his tattered foot.

"Then what?" he said tersely.

"I'll repair your foot," said Tulip, "and I'll find somewhere more convenient to hide our worldly wealth."

"You have needle and thread all to hand?" said Magnus in a heavily sarcastic voice.

"Naturally," said his wife, picking up a card of purple cotton from the parcel. Two needles of different sizes were slotted into it. "It's not much use thinking at all, if you don't think of everything!"

She took Joshua's coat from the wardrobe and went downstairs.

CHAPTER 8

Joshua

It was dark when Joshua opened the front door and slipped out into the silent street. He looked about him, saw the broad walkway the other side of the road, beyond which was the river. Downstream were the lights on the bridges and in the city, but here was darkness that the lamps were too weak to conquer. Even the globes on the promenade did no more than give a fairy glow.

Joshua made sure that the street was really deserted. Then he stepped out of the doorway of Number 39 and turned left to see who or what occupied the ground floor.

It was a shop. Shutters of heavy wire mesh covered the glass. Joshua peered through into a space that was lit only faintly by the street lamp on the corner. He stepped back sharply as he saw someone sitting there at what looked like a sewing machine. But in an instant he realised that the figure was some sort of dummy. His eyes became accustomed to the gloom and he made out other things – tables, chairs and an assortment of small furniture.

A secondhand shop, he thought, or maybe an antique dealer's. More than likely, something in between. The owner could be some sort of collector. And rag dolls, he thought wryly, might well be considered collectable.

He crossed to the other side of the road and looked up at the shop sign. It was very difficult to make out by lamplight, but it looked like "I", or maybe "L", "& P. *Waggons*". The shop had a broad frontage with a big window either side of the doorway. To the right hand side of it, a short lane ran steeply up towards the town. It was a cobbled street with a narrow pavement either side.

Joshua turned up the lane. The riverside was left behind him and, walking quickly, he soon found himself on more familiar ground. Cutting through an alleyway, he rejoined the main road again and came to the railway viaduct. Half way up the hill, he turned right, onto a steep flight of steps between high buildings that led up to the Market Place. From there he crossed into the High Street where the shop of a Shell Station was open late and had, thank goodness, a rack of newspapers near the pay window. Joshua selected two of them and handed over the right money. ·

"Not a bad night," said the man in the kiosk. "Quite summery."

"Not bad for May," said Joshua, his head down looking at the date on the newspaper. He hurried away, well pleased that much less than a year had passed since last he had walked the streets of Castledean. He was eager to get back to North Shore Road to let his mother know, but his mission was not yet complete. There was still very important work to do. He left the garage, crossed the High Street and walked down to Brocklehurst Grove.

When he came to the front gate he looked in at the garden. Even at this hour of the night he could tell that no gardener was tending it. The hedge was reaching over the wall into the street. Weeds were growing up the gate-posts. The house beyond was in total darkness. There was surely nobody living there. But was Soobie still inside?

Joshua stepped back onto the green and craned his neck to

inspect the windows in the roof of Number 5, in case there might be a light there. A light in the attic, he reasoned, and nowhere else in the house, would surely mean that Soobie was still up there. Vain hope! The windows in the roof were invisible in the darkness.

He went back to the gate and, with some hesitation, he opened it and walked slowly up the familiar path. He found himself longing for a return to the old order. I was so content with things as they were, he thought. If only I could be back in my old nightwatchman's job at Sydenham's, pretending to drink chocolate from my Port Vale mug . . . that would be happiness.

He looked at the front of the house and had not the faintest idea what to do next. Without keys, he could not enter. To ring the doorbell would be pointless if no one answered, perhaps disastrous if anyone did! But suppose Soobie was still inside, just Soobie?

Joshua went close to the lounge window and put his face against the glass. The curtains were not closed. That must mean something. But to see anything through the nets in such darkness was impossible.

Joshua decided to make his way to the back of the house. He stayed close to the wall and followed the path up the lefthand side, past the windows of the nursery and the breakfast-room, coming at length to the kitchen and the back door. He looked up at the back of the house. There was even less to see than at the front because there was no light from anywhere. The curtains, as far as he could see, were just as the Mennyms had left them – not too wide open, but not closed enough to look odd in daytime.

Joshua walked right round the building, returning to the front door from the opposite direction. He stood a while longer. Then he made up his mind. He gave two sharp rings on the doorbell, heard them echo through the empty house and trembled. For a minute he waited. Nothing happened. He rang again, more boldly, and stepped back to look up at the windows. No one came.

Joshua left the garden and walked quickly out of the street. His heart was weighed down with sadness because he had not found Soobie and he did not know what more he could do.

He was making his way back to the riverside when he remembered one other thing Tulip had asked him to undertake. In his pocket was the bank card. "If the year is not up," she had said, "find a cash machine. Take out two hundred pounds. That will serve so many purposes. I will know that everything is in working order. The bank will know that I am still using my account. And we shall have more cash in hand."

He went to the machine outside the bank in Deacon Street, pressed all the right buttons, and was given a handful of notes. Tulip would be pleased. But Vinetta? Vinetta would be heartbroken. Her husband was returning home with no word of their son.

CHAPTER 9

Meanwhile . . .

When Joshua left the house, the others began to disperse. Poopie was the first to go. He made a brief foray into the nursery and then went back to his own room with his prize. No matter what any of them might say about leaving everything as they found it, there was no way he was going to let Googles keep *his* rabbit. He had spotted it in the playpen whilst they were searching the house for Soobie and had been silently indignant. That rabbit was *his*. It was not a toy! It was part of an elaborate pretend – a real, pretend rabbit called Paddy Black who was Poopie's own pet. Poopie stroked its head, smoothed back its long ears and gave it a good talking to.

"I can't turn my back on you," he said. "What d'you want to go and get in the playpen for? Googles could pull you to bits. She wouldn't mean it. She's just a baby. But you can't trust babies with animals. You should have the sense to know that."

Miss Quigley knew all about the limitations of babies.

"I don't know how I'll manage to get Googles to stay still and be quiet if anyone comes," she said with a worried look at Vinetta and Tulip.

"I could stitch her lips together," said Tulip in a voice that

50

sounded as if she meant it, though of course she didn't. "I have got a needle and thread."

Vinetta and Hortensia looked horrified.

"You can't mean that, Tulip," said Vinetta. "It would be barbaric."

"Well," said Tulip, "what I do mean is that you have a problem and you will have to solve it somehow. There's no 'if' about it. Somebody will come. And when they do, Googles will have to be as stiff and as silent as the rest of us. You'll have to manage it — one way, or another. Now, I must go back to Magnus. You can both stay down here and start training the baby to stay still in your arms."

"She wasn't in my arms," said Miss Quigley with growing consternation. "She was in the playpen."

"Difficult," said Tulip, "but if it takes you all the hours between now and Monday morning, you'll have to do it."

"But the baby needs her sleep," said Miss Quigley, unable so easily to abandon a deeply-ingrained pretend.

"Not that baby," said Tulip maliciously. "You must not allow her to sleep till she understands fully what is expected of her. Otherwise, well otherwise, who knows what I might have to do!"

Miss Quigley drew herself up to her full height and clutched Googles protectively. When she spoke her words were brief but definite.

"By tomorrow," she said, "Googles will have learnt a new trick. I shall say the word and she will be totally still and silent."

With that she swept off to the nursery. How she was going to manage to do it, she did not know, but do it she would. No one, no one, could be allowed to harm the most precious baby on the planet!

Vinetta followed her.

Appleby gave a sigh of relief after they had gone. Wimpey

51

was sitting on the window ledge, hidden by the curtain, looking out onto the street and watching for her father to return. Appleby and Pilbeam were left virtually alone together. It was the chance that Appleby had been waiting for. She moved her chair closer to Pilbeam's and, in a quiet voice, began to ask all the questions she had been bottling up for the past few hours.

"Now tell me everything," she said. "I want to know everything that has happened from the moment the door in the attic closed again."

"That was well over two years ago," said Pilbeam. "There's a lot to tell. You were dead for two years."

"And you were not living for forty," said Appleby irritably, reminding her sister that she had remained an unfinished doll in the attic at Brocklehurst Grove till Soobie discovered her and Vinetta brought her to life. It was something that was mostly forgotten and that Pilbeam preferred to pretend had never happened.

It was a hurtful thing to say, but Pilbeam glossed over it. She understood Appleby better than any of them and usually she knew how to keep her in check. But this was different. Pilbeam was simply overjoyed that her sister, who was also her best friend, was living again, faults and all.

All the while they were talking in low tones, Wimpey sat behind the curtain and gazed down at the street. It was interesting, even though the place was deserted. It was almost exciting. Looking straight ahead, she could see on the other side of the dark road the globes that lit the promenade. To her left, she could see the lights on the bridges, especially the Dean Bridge with its elegant arch. At intervals, she saw trains cross the upper level of the Victoria Bridge, and across the black sky came the occasional flicker of an aeroplane's lights as it headed for the airport. It was, she thought guiltily, much more interesting than Brocklehurst Grove!

The hours crept by, but Wimpey remained awake and attentive. Then, just as her interest was beginning to flag, she looked along the street and gave a great gasp as she saw something, someone . . .

"Soobie!" she yelled. "Mum! Granny! Everybody! Look! Look! Look!"

Under the streetlamp on the corner, she had seen her brother in his blue tracksuit, jogging along, looking swiftly to his left and right. It was him, she knew it was.

But by the time her sisters came to the window, carefully pulling the curtains round their shoulders, the runner was out of sight.

"There's no one there," said Appleby, irritated at being disturbed. "You've imagined it."

"I didn't. Honest I didn't," said Wimpey, turning to Pilbeam for support. They went back into the room. Vinetta came in from the nursery to see what the shouting was about. Wimpey was upset at not being believed, and overwrought and overtired. Vinetta took her on her knee and gently stroked her hair. Ten is definitely not too old to be nursed, if the occasion calls for nursing.

"You did see someone running," said Vinetta. "I'm sure you did. But it might have been anyone. Soobie is not the only one who goes jogging at night."

"It was Soobie," Wimpey persisted. "I know it was."

"It might have been," sighed her mother. "We have no way of knowing."

At that moment there was a tap at the front door. Joshua had returned with the newspapers, the money and the news that Soobie was nowhere to be seen.

CHAPTER 10

Deductions and Decisions

"What are we going to do?" said Vinetta. "He must be *somewhere*."

All the business of newspapers and money was just so much trivia compared with her anxiety over Soobie. Vinetta was not so easily distracted from what to her was the main issue.

Wimpey snuggled up to her. She listened without understanding to Tulip's plans for putting all things in motion to retrieve the family's savings. She heard Pilbeam and Appleby commenting on articles in the newspapers, scattering sheets across the furniture. New knowledge came in a jumbled heap. But Wimpey knew what was most important to her mother, and Wimpey knew that she really had seen Soobie.

"He was outside, Mum," she said. "I know he was. I saw him. He was jogging."

The word "jogging" acted as an inspiration for Appleby.

"He would be," she said, looking up from the page she was reading. "He always goes jogging late at night. That will be why he wasn't in when Dad rang the bell."

"You really think that?" said Vinetta eagerly. Joshua also considered this idea, and nodded.

"It seems logical," said Appleby. "I mean – he's not

at home, and Wimpey did see *someone*. We've no way of knowing how much Soobie has managed to find out. It is possible that he has some idea of our whereabouts."

"But he didn't find us," said Pilbeam. "So what would he do next?"

"He'd go back to the Grove," said Joshua. "That's what I would do. He'd go back to the Grove and try to work things out. Then he'll search again tomorrow night."

"But next time," said Vinetta, "we will be watching for him."

"But *he* won't know that," said Tulip.

Those words, so simple in themselves, gave Vinetta a crushing picture of her eldest son, sitting in an empty house, not knowing which way to turn.

"You'll have to go back," she said, turning to her husband. "Go straightaway, Josh, and ring the bell again."

She had no regard at all for the fact that Joshua had already spent ages roaming round the town. When it came to her children's welfare, she spared no one. Joshua felt trapped. The effort of walking, after months of sitting stiff and still, had made him feel genuinely exhausted. He wanted to sit quiet in the armchair for a few hours. The voices of his family, all talking at once, grated on his nerves. There were plenty of beds in the house. Could they not all just go to bed?

"It's too late," he said. "It's too far to go. By the time I returned it would be daylight – for all *we* know, there could be somebody here, wondering where I am."

Vinetta was about to argue, but Pilbeam came up with another idea.

"The phone might still be working," said Pilbeam. "Even if the new people have taken it over, the number is probably the same. We could try ringing Soobie."

"I'll do that," said Appleby. "There's a phone box along

the street. I noticed it when we were looking out of the window."

"No," said Tulip firmly. "If anyone goes it will have to be Joshua. Young girls do not go out at this time of night."

Appleby pulled a face but said no more.

"What will you do if a stranger answers?" said Vinetta to Joshua, taking it for granted that he would be going to the phone immediately.

"He'll just have to say he's got a wrong number," said Appleby.

Then Vinetta thought of another difficulty.

"Soobie won't answer," she said. "He won't know who's ringing."

"At this time in the morning? He'll have a good idea. He's no fool," said Appleby. "He might ignore it at first, but if it persists he will answer."

Pilbeam saw the sense of this.

"You may have to ring more than once," she said. "Let it ring for a time. Then stop. Then ring again and let it ring for a long time. And keep on doing that till you get a reply."

"What if he's not there?" said Joshua.

"He will be," said Pilbeam, suddenly sure of what her twin would do, not guessing but knowing instinctively. "It will be just as you said, Father. He'll be there from sunrise till sunset. Then he'll come out again to try and find us."

Wearily, Joshua took his coat off the back of the chair and put it on again.

"I'll need some change," he said. Then added, "I hope the phone box isn't vandalised."

"If it is," said Vinetta, "you'll have to find another one."

What she meant was – don't return till you have spoken to Soobie!

CHAPTER 11

Hello?

Brrrrr . . . brrrr . . . brrr . . .

Soobie jumped in terror. The shock was so great he nearly burst every seam on his body. His crinkly blue hair stiffened like the hair on the back of a startled dog. There he was, methodically securing the back door in a silent house when the silence was shattered by a ringing he did not immediately identify as the telephone. He had just returned from his jog to North Shore Road. He locked up and put the key in his pocket, the safest place for it. He fastened two bolts and was bending down to fasten the third.

Then brrrrr . . . brrrr . . . brrr . . .

There were two telephones in Number 5 Brocklehurst Grove. There always had been, for reasons the Mennyms never knew. The house had been Kate Penshaw's own home for the whole of her life. The telephones were part of the Mennyms' inheritance. One was in the big front bedroom. The other was in the breakfast-room, next to the kitchen.

Soobie slid the third bolt into place quickly, stood up and listened. He knew now that it was the telephone ringing, but as suddenly as it started, it stopped. Who would be ringing an empty house in the early hours of a Sunday morning?

When the ringing stopped, Soobie decided that it must be

a wrong number. There could be no other explanation. He settled back into himself and became calm.

Then . . .

Brrrrr . . . brrrr . . . brrr . . .

It started again.

Soobie went into the breakfast-room. A hint of the coming day made the room's contours perceptible, the bare floor boards, the light fixture in the centre of the ceiling, the partly-drawn curtains. On the window ledge, in the centre, was the big, old-fashioned black telephone. It sat there ringing insistently.

It must be a wrong number. It must be!

To pick up the receiver would serve no purpose at all. It might even be dangerous. It was difficult in that instant to think logically.

In the telephone box on North Shore Road, Joshua let the phone go dead again, took the coin that fell from the slot and reinserted it ready to try once more . . . twice more, or three times more if need be . . . as many times as it might take. At least it was ringing. At least he knew that the number still existed. There was no way he was going to return empty-handed to Vinetta. By now he was convinced that Soobie would be in Brocklehurst Grove hearing the phone ring, and ignoring it.

Oh, Soobie, he thought, why do you have to be so careful?

From the telephone box, Joshua could see the windows of the flat. He could not see Vinetta and the others watching him, but he knew that they were there. They had turned out the light so that they would not be seen peering round the curtains. Joshua kept a look out all around him. The telephone box was not inconspicuous enough for his liking. But the road remained eerily deserted and in the buildings all along the street there was no sign of life.

The phone had rung three times when Soobie began to think, that call could be for me. Each ring lasted longer than the one before. The persistence began to seem meaningful. It could be one of the family trying to get in touch, thought Soobie. But how would they manage to ring him? Where would the phone be? Surely it would require a great leap of imagination for them to believe that *he* was there, ready to answer their call?

The next time the phone rang, Soobie took courage, grabbed the receiver, and put it firmly to his ear.

"Hello?" he said. His tone was edged with suspicion and unnaturally sharp.

Joshua heard the voice and was almost sure who it was, but not entirely. He paused to think.

"Hello," he said tentatively.

Soobie thought he recognised his father's voice, but couldn't swear to it.

"Hello?" he said again.

Joshua was still unsure and unwilling to declare himself.

"Hello," he said.

Soobie began to think that this was, after all, some stranger playing stupid games.

"Hello," he said brusquely. "What is it you want?"

Soobie's voice was strained with tension and down the telephone line he ceased to sound like himself at all. Joshua was tempted to put the phone down, but the thought of Vinetta made him hang on.

He opened his mouth to say "Hello" yet again, but then he thought, this is daft, we could go on like this all night. So he decided to take a chance. He would ask for Soobie. If the person at the other end of the line did not

59

recognise the name, so what? Everybody gets wrong numbers sometimes.

"Soobie," he said, "is that you?"

"Dad!" said Soobie joyfully. "Am I glad to hear your voice! Where are you? Where is everybody?"

There are no words to convey how relieved Joshua was at that moment. He stood dumb for so long that Soobie looked down anxiously at the handset and wondered if the phone had gone dead.

"Dad," he said urgently. "Tell me where you all are. Tell me what to do next."

That was more like it. That was practical.

"Stay where you are, son. Tell me all you can, but don't do anything rash. We're still feeling our way down here. We don't know ourselves what is going to happen."

Joshua put two more coins in the slot.

They gave each other all the information they could. Soobie gasped when he was told of Appleby's revival, then realised that his plea for *all of us* had been taken more literally than he could ever have hoped for.

"So it *was* you that Wimpey saw from the window!" said Joshua when Soobie had told him about jogging down to North Shore Road.

"It looks as if I might be brought down to the flat myself on Saturday," said Soobie, "though I don't know for sure. But Saturday's a long way off. Can't I sneak in and see you before then?"

That idea filled Joshua with misgiving. It sounded much too risky. But he tried to think what Vinetta might say and he came up with a compromise.

"You won't be able to come out in daylight," he said. "You never have. It is almost morning now. We don't know for sure when the people who put us in the flat at Number 39 will be back. So for now just stay where you are. I will ring you again after dark this evening. By then we may know more."

There was a long pause before Soobie answered.

"If I don't hear from you," he then said with decision, "I'm coming down there anyway. Nothing will happen here before Saturday. I'm not sitting alone in the attic for another week. I can sneak out and sneak in every night if I want to. And I want to!"

CHAPTER 12

Reunion

"He's coming," said Wimpey excitedly. "I can see him. He's just come round the corner."

She had her face pressed against the glass and was straining to look sideways along the street. Soobie disappeared from sight again beneath the windows, and then the doorbell rang. Poopie, who was nearest, ran down the front stairs. Before anyone could advise caution, he reached up to the Yale lock, turned it easily, and opened the door.

"Soobie!" he shouted as he saw his brother standing on the doorstep, head bent, face hidden. Joshua, on the staircase, winced at Poopie's recklessness. True, it was ten o'clock on Sunday night and the whole neighbourhood was deserted, and had been more or less deserted all day, but it always pays to be careful.

"Come in quickly and shut the door as softly as you can," he said in an urgent but quiet voice.

Joshua had tried to persuade Soobie not to come at all, to wait till they knew more of what was happening. But Soobie had refused to listen. He had every confidence in his own ability to travel by night, and he was determined to see his family again as soon as possible. Now he followed his father and Poopie upstairs and into the living-room and stood among them all, feeling awkward, but deeply glad to be there. In all the time he had spent sitting still in the attic, he had never dared to hope for an outcome such as this. He placed one hand on his mother's arm. Then he looked at Appleby. Her gaze met his. Each was delighted to see the other, but neither quite knew what to say.

Vinetta understood.

"Sit down," she said to Soobie. "You've come a long way. You must need a rest. I'll make us all a cup of tea. Then we can swop stories."

At these words, they all became more relaxed. Somehow the notion of tea made the present situation less frightening. If they could have pretend tea, if Vinetta could behave as if everything were normal, perhaps things wouldn't be too bad after all.

In a short time, Vinetta returned from the kitchen carrying a tray she had managed to find, with a plate and four mugs on it. She handed one mug to Soobie who took it with as much grace as he could muster. Throughout his life he had hated pretends, but this one was meant to be a comfort, and, in its way, it was, even for him.

Vinetta handed a mug to Tulip. The third mug was given to Appleby, whose special status gave her some priority. Pilbeam, with a little of her twin's reluctance, accepted the last one.

"You and I will have to make do with pretend mugs," Vinetta said quite seriously to Joshua, handing him a mug that wasn't there, which he took with his usual aplomb. Then he held emptiness cupped in his hands as if it were solid ware, kiln-baked.

"I've poured you two a glass of lemonade," she said to Poopie and Wimpey. She carefully gave them each an invisible glass which they grasped realistically.

"Mind you don't spill it," she said.

Wimpey, entering into the spirit of things, said, "Whoops!" and wiped some drops from her skirt.

By the time all the tales had been told, it was past midnight. Miss Quigley had not put in an appearance. She and the baby were out of sight and out of mind. Tulip had been up to tell Sir Magnus that Soobie had arrived and she relayed all that was happening on the floor below.

"He'll have to go back before daylight," said Magnus. "No good him staying here. Heaven alone knows what will be happening tomorrow."

"He knows that, Magnus," said Tulip. "He's not stupid."

Soobie sat in the chair where Pilbeam had been sitting and let himself become familiar with the room, noting that practically all of the furniture had come from their old home. He had less to say for himself than any of the others, except maybe Joshua, but in the general hubbub his silences were never noticed. One thing a group of Mennyms can do from dusk till dawn and back again is talk.

But as the pointers of the clock on the shelf, agreeing with Soobie's watch, approached twelve-thirty, Vinetta suddenly became aware that the younger twins were looking and sounding very sleepy. Sleeping at night had begun so long ago that no one remembered the beginning.

Saturday night had been an exception. They had all just come back to life in such strange surroundings that they forgot all about going to bed and sleeping. Except for Sir Magnus, who was already in bed, no one had slept at all since then. The older Mennyms found it easy to go without sleep, but the younger ones were so used to being sent to bed early that the habit was hard to conquer. Now that the first excitement was over, yawning and nodding became the order of the day.

"I think you two should go to bed," said Vinetta in her most motherly voice. "You will have to be up very early in the morning, but at least you can have a few hours rest."

Poopie had come back to life with his shoulders resting against a bed in a room full of his own belongings. That was obviously intended to be his own room. It was clear to him where he should sleep.

Wimpey was not so sure.

"Where is my bed?" she asked.

"The room with three beds must be the girls' room," said Vinetta. "You will have a bed in there."

"Any bed?" said Wimpey.

"Not the one near the window," said Appleby quickly. "If I go to bed at all in this place, that bed will have to be mine."

Appleby by now knew the flat from top to bottom. She knew that in the girls' room, where many of her own clothes were stored, was a bed close to the window.

"Perhaps you should go to bed now too," said Vinetta.

"No," said Appleby. "Definitely not."

She had missed enough already. If they talked the clock around again, she would be there to listen.

CHAPTER 13

Play Dead

When the younger twins had gone to bed, the rest of the family continued to mull over the uncertainties of their present position.

"As I see it," said Tulip, "we must live from day to day, from hour to hour, till we know what the owner of this house has in mind for us. Patience is everything."

"Well, at least tomorrow is Monday. We shouldn't have to be patient for long," said Joshua.

The others looked towards him. His pipe was firmly clasped again, the stem pointing decisively to the ceiling in the manner of the great detective.

"The shop downstairs should be open then," he said. "Its owners must surely own this flat. They will be the people who had us brought here and who fixed up this place using the furniture from Brocklehurst Grove. The woman Soobie calls Daisy has to fit in somewhere. She probably owns both the flat and the shop. It's not an unreasonable assumption."

"But just think how frightening tomorrow is going to be, and how alert and quiet we shall have to be all day long," said Vinetta, trying to get her mind around the idea. "Anything that happens is likely to be something for the worse. There'll be so many things to be careful of."

"We'll be prepared," said Tulip firmly. "I know precisely where I was when I returned to life – sitting in the armchair upstairs, holding in my hands an ugly piece of pink knitting. Magnus was in his bed, propped up by pillows and reading a book. You must all know where you were at the moment you awoke. From early in the morning we'll take turns being on guard in the hall and as soon as there is the least sound at the front door we'll prepare to freeze in positions as near exact as we can manage."

"I haven't seen Miss Quigley," said Soobie. "Shouldn't she be in on this? If you're all planning what to do, so should she."

"Oh!" said Vinetta guiltily. "I forgot all about Hortensia! Soobie's coming put her out of my mind. She's in the nursery with Googles. She did ask us not to disturb her."

As if on cue, Hortensia appeared at the living room door.

"If you and Lady Mennym would like to come next door," she said proudly, looking at Vinetta, "I have something to show you."

They all followed her to the nursery, Tulip leading the way.

Googles was sitting in the playpen jiggling the ball with the carousel inside and saying, "Ah . . . babba . . . goya . . . goya . . . goya." Miss Quigley smiled down at her and said firmly, "Play dead."

Googles carefully placed the ball in the centre of the playpen, sat with her back against the corner post and let her arms go stiff to either side of her. Her little face beneath its kiss-curl became a perfect blank.

"There," said Miss Quigley, looking very smugly at Tulip, "that should be satisfactory."

"Most impressive," said Tulip. "How do you unfreeze her again?"

"I pick her up and cuddle her," said Hortensia. "She knows that. It's part of the game."

Hortensia bent over the side of the playpen, lifted her charge up in her arms, and Googles came delightfully and gleefully back to life.

"Let me try," said Tulip, taking the baby from her nanny's arms and sitting her down in the playpen again. Googles beat the ball with the flat of her hands and cooed.

"Play dead," said Tulip.

Googles looked up at her, laughed, and rolled the ball across the playpen floor.

Tulip gave Miss Quigley a mocking look.

"That's not much good," she said. "This new trick of yours will have to work every time."

"Play dead," said Hortensia quite gently. Googles repeated her earlier performance to perfection.

"It does work – every single time," said her nanny, "but only when I say the words. She returns to life only when I lift her up. She is just a baby after all. I think she has done brilliantly well to have learnt so much."

Soobie, standing in the doorway applauded, though naturally cloth hands clapping make little noise. Still, his expression of approval was clearly visible and Miss Quigley, suddenly noticing for the first time that he was of their company, appreciated it. She gave him a glad smile, but said nothing. To ask too many questions was not in her nature. It would, indeed, have seemed to her impertinent.

"Now," said Soobie, when they returned to the living room, "I will have to go back to the Grove. Ring me tomorrow evening, Father, and bring me up to date with whatever happens in the morning. I'll be here again tomorrow night unless there is some strong reason why I cannot come."

CHAPTER 14

Upstairs . . .

Eventually, all of the Mennyms retired to bed. It was a way of passing the time till morning came. But they were up and ready long before it was necessary. It was Joshua who decided that it should be a six o'clock start.

"The big cupboard next to the kitchen is full of stuff," he said, "and the attics are crammed with furniture and crates and boxes."

"So?" said Vinetta. "Whoever owns this house must have stored them away."

"There's far too much for it to be ordinary household lumber. The shop downstairs is some sort of antique dealer's. Those rooms must be store-rooms. We don't know what time the shop opens. What is worse, we don't know whether the owner will be coming up here before opening time for more stock."

So it was action stations, check everything, and be ready to freeze at a moment's notice. But seven, eight and nine o'clock arrived and nothing happened. Vehicles passed along the street. Pedestrians came in ones and twos. But no one even paused at the shop.

Then, at a quarter to ten . . . activity. Two men came to the shop front, removed the shutters and carried them round the corner to the back of the building with an adroitness and speed that showed that this must be the customary beginning to the working day.

At five to ten a taxi drew up. Its driver got out and opened the door for his passenger, which gave her the air of being a Very Important Person.

The watchers in the room above saw the top of an elderly woman's head with its neat grey hair. Even the foreshortened view they had of her left them in no doubt that she was an unusually short woman with broad shoulders. As she stepped from the taxi onto the pavement they observed that she was supporting herself with a stick.

The taxi driver was paid and drove away. The men who had removed the shutters returned to the front of the shop where they held a short conversation with the newcomer before walking off in the direction of the bridges.

"See you at tea-time then," one of them called as he waved his hand. That was all the Mennyms heard, but it was enough to give them some idea of the pattern of the day. The woman disappeared into the shop and the watchers were aware of the faint tinkle of the bell over the door.

From time to time that morning they heard the telephone ringing in the shop below and they heard the occupant moving around; not that she was noisy or that the phone was allowed to ring for long, but the listeners were silent and very attentive. When they spoke to each other they did so in whispers. When they themselves moved it was with breathless caution.

Tulip had gone upstairs to sit in the chair by Sir Magnus's bed as soon as the men arrived to take down the shutters. Joshua had placed himself strategically on the landing keeping his eyes fixed on the front door, waiting for the knob to turn on the lock, poised to return to his seat in the living room the minute it did. Neither he nor his mother saw the shopkeeper arrive in her taxi, but other members of the family kept them informed, moving as swiftly and silently as possible, then returning to their proper positions.

After an hour or so, they all began to suspect that the danger of someone coming up to see them was not so imminent. They relaxed, but only slightly. Tulip came downstairs again. Joshua took a stool out onto the landing, feeling confident that he would be able to return it in good time should the door eventually be opened.

"If the woman in the shop downstairs needs a stick to walk with," said Tulip, "she won't be able to run up those stairs in a hurry. It'll be a wonder to me if she can manage it at all. I hope this ten o'clock start is routine and not just a Monday morning effort. It will simplify my job if I can count on being able to go out early one of these days."

She was sitting close to Vinetta on a dining chair that would have to be returned to its proper place at the table should the warning come.

"What do you mean?" said Vinetta with a puzzled look at the sharp crystal eyes of her mother-in-law.

"There's the bank to see to, for a start, and the building societies. Though perhaps I should contact our solicitor first."

Vinetta gasped. She knew that Tulip had plans to regain the family's money, but she had no idea that her mother-in-law intended to make expeditions into the outside world. Money from the machine, yes, obtained by Joshua. Sending letters was also possible. But for Tulip to go out in broad daylight seemed a risk too great to contemplate.

"As soon as it seems feasible to do so, I shall go to the phone box some morning and ring Rothwell and Ramshaw," continued Tulip. "Their Mr Dobb is the soul of discretion. I will be able to make all sorts of arrangements with him."

She kept her voice down and spoke only to Vinetta. "That

will be the first step. I'm not saying it will be possible this week or even next week, but I do have five months in hand. It is only seven months since I deposited the letters."

"But what's the use?" asked Vinetta. "We're stuck here. The money wouldn't help even if we could get our hands on it. I can't see any way out."

"I can," said Tulip firmly. "It may seem like a pinpoint of light at the end of an amazingly long tunnel. But keep faith, Vinetta. It *is* there."

CHAPTER 15

. . . And Downstairs

The woman in the shop below was Daisy Maughan, the owner of an antique business and the guardian of a newly acquired family of life-sized rag dolls. She called them 'the Mennyms', for that was the name of the people who claimed to have cared for them, the people who for more than forty years had been the tenants of Number 5 Brocklehurst Grove.

Daisy had been asked to take on the task of emptying the house after 'the Mennyms' had apparently departed with mysterious and unexplained speed, leaving behind all their possessions and a room full of rag dolls. A letter found with the dolls consigned their care to whoever owned the house. It claimed to be a directive given by Kate Penshaw and faithfully observed for forty-seven years by her 'tenants', who now passed on both the letter and the responsibility.

The new owner was Jennifer Gladstone, Lorna's mother – and Albert's mother-in-law. Jennifer, alarmed at the dolls' lifelike appearance, refused to have anything to do with them. So Lorna took over and promised to find a solution to the problem.

It was Albert who remembered the shop by the riverside. After that everything fell into place. Daisy inspected the house she was to empty, saw the dolls, loved them, and made a home for them in the flat above her shop.

Daisy Maughan ran the shop called L & P WAGGONS all on her own. It was principally an antique shop but it also sold theatrical costumes and various curiosities that could not quite carry the label 'antique'. She had inherited the business from her father; it was a living thing that had changed with the years.

Daisy went into the shop and hung her coat on its usual peg. Then she took a duster to the furniture, beginning with the octagonal table that served as her desk and then checking methodically on all of her wares in the left-hand window, finishing with a visit to the large wooden betty doll seated at the treadle sewing machine in the corner. It was as big as a dummy in a clothes shop window, but there the resemblance ended. The doll with its grained wood face and painted-on lips and eyes was so familiar to Daisy that it had become like an old friend. She was dressed in Victorian clothes and her hair, as wooden as the rest of her, was drawn back into a bun.

"Well, Lily," said Daisy to the doll, "it should be an interesting day today. Soon as the shop's closed, I'll be up to see my new family. Not that I care any the less for you, mind, but you can never have too many friends."

When the articles in the right-hand window had been freshened up and the theatrical costumes there checked for dust, Daisy spoke in like fashion to another doll, sister to the first, who sat at an ancient typewriter with her spindly fingers on the keyboard.

"It looks like being another fine day, Polly," she said. "I might even have to pull down the sunblind. It's a wonderful May we're having, isn't it?"

These dolls were called Lily and Polly because Daisy

74

thought of them as being the L & P Waggons named on the board above the shopfront, for no one knew who the original Waggons were and when, if ever, they had been the owners of the shop. And no one knew where the wooden dolls had come from.

At ten-thirty the shop was open to the public. Daisy had collected her mail from the doormat and was sitting at the octagonal table sorting through it, ready for any customers who might arrive. On a shelf behind her, in easy reach, was the telephone. It rang two or three times in the course of the next hour. Many of Daisy's customers came by arrangement with specific purchases in mind. Hers was a well-respected business run with great care and efficiency.

Daisy had only three real customers before lunch and two or three who were 'just looking'. At lunchtime, she shut up shop, went into the little kitchen at the back and made herself a pot of tea to go with the sandwiches she had brought from home.

"It's not been a bad morning," she said, talking to herself again. "I'm glad Mrs Woodhouse eventually took the candlesticks. I have never known a woman take so long to make up her mind!"

In the afternoon one customer bought a carved sideboard. That was the major sale of the day, but the major sales were what kept the minor ones going.

"I think I'll close early," said Daisy, looking at her watch. It was a quarter to five. "Nobody comes in this late without ringing up first. And I daresay Ted and Michael will not mind being a bit prompt with the shutters."

She rang her helpers and they came straight along. Theirs was an odd-job and small-removal business. Daisy had for years been their favourite customer. They did her deliveries, helped with her storage, and took care of the shutters that were now an obligatory part of running a shop in Castledean, a sad sign of the times.

"Had enough for one day?" said Ted.

"Or made enough?" joked Michael.

"A bit of both," laughed Daisy. "I won't be going out of business yet! Neither will you – there's a sideboard to deliver this week."

CHAPTER 16

First Encounter

Step ... clump. Step ... clump. Step ... clump. Step
... clump.

The sound of the halting footsteps on the stairs reached
every room in the flat.

The Mennyms had heard the door below open. By the time
it closed again, each one of them was back in place. It was as if
they had never come to life at all. Poopie was in the bedroom,
sitting with his back against the bed, looking fixedly at the
rebuilt training tower. In the room next door, Magnus was
resting against his pillows, reading his one and only book.
Tulip, in her armchair, sat with her elbows correctly bent
holding the needles with the pink knitting.

In the room below, Joshua, Vinetta, Pilbeam and Appleby
were in their proper chairs looking blankly at the blank screen
of the television set. Wimpey sat cross-legged on the floor
in front of her mother, nursing her doll and feeling very
apprehensive.

Miss Quigley, in the nursery, had lifted a finger to her
lips as a first indication to Googles that silence and stillness
were about to begin. Googles smiled, put one hand over her
mouth, then reached out for the ball. Her nanny shook her
head vigorously and Googles sat up straight again.

"Play dead," said Miss Quigley, and Googles obediently set her back against the post of the playpen and stretched out her arms to either side as if they were incapable of bending. She did it so wonderfully well that it was all her nanny could do to stop herself picking the baby up in her arms and giving her the cuddle she surely deserved.

The footsteps stopped. There was a tap at the living-room door followed by a slight pause before it opened. Then their visitor stood in the doorway, smiling at all of them in friendly fashion.

"Hello, everybody," she said to a startled though rigid audience. "Daisy's come to see you at long last. How did you enjoy the weekend?"

So this was Daisy!

The Mennyms were flabbergasted. The room became charged as if they had all screamed out in a voice whose pitch was too high to be heard. This newcomer, this newcomer, was talking to them! Talking to them as if she knew they could hear! The thrill of it was enough to paralyse. So it was not difficult to remain outwardly passive. That first moment was the danger point and sheer terror took them through it.

Daisy came right into the room. In one hand she held her walking stick which she stood in the corner by the door. Under her arm she was carrying a shallow, rectangular cardboard box. She put it down till she removed her coat, then she took it to the television set.

"I thought we might watch the telly for a while," she said, "but that circular aerial is impossible. I've brought a horizontal one that might improve things."

She bent down and switched on the set, shaking her head as the picture appeared shot with snowy streaks. Five pairs of button eyes bored into the back of her neck.

"Impossible," she said again. Then she unpacked the new aerial, unplugged the old one, sat down gingerly on the floor beside Wimpey, and set about fine-tuning the stations. The image on the screen became clearer and the sound became crisper.

"There," she said, looking over her shoulder at Joshua. "I bet you thought I couldn't do that! I'm sixty-eight you know, and I've never been one of the fittest. But they do say cracked pots last the longest!"

She got up awkwardly, using an arm of Appleby's chair for support. Then she pulled forward a dining chair from the table and sat next to Vinetta.

"No," she said, again looking at Joshua, "don't get up. I really prefer a hard-backed chair. It gives me more support."

They all sat through a programme about cacti. It told the strange, almost sad story of the Century Plant, *Agave Americana*, cherished by gardeners who feel privileged to see it bloom just once in a lifetime.

"Amazing, isn't it?" said Daisy. "Imagine a plant that takes a hundred years to produce a flower! And it's not even an oak tree, just a cactus no more than three feet high!"

Wimpey, in momentary forgetfulness, tilted her head back to look more closely at the picture. Her mother, observing, was alarmed, but Daisy did not move her eyes from the screen.

As they all sat there, the Mennyms passed from fear to bafflement to the glimmer of understanding. Vinetta began to realise that Daisy did not, could not, know that her companions were hearing every word she said. Appleby, coming to a similar conclusion, had to hold back a giggle.

The aerial needed adjusting slightly when Daisy changed channels for the news.

"Still," she said, this time looking at Appleby and Pilbeam, "it's not too bad. A roof aerial would be better, but this'll do for now."

She sat back in her chair again and then did a very 'Mennym' thing. She ignored the newsreader's efforts to make known the events of the world, and began to talk.

"I used to live in this flat, you know," she said, looking at Vinetta and talking woman to woman. "That was years and years ago, when my mam and dad were alive. We didn't have TV then. That's why there's no outside aerial. We got our first set when we moved to Glenthorn Drive."

Scientists in Nova Scotia are testing out a new theory to explain the temperature changes that have given rise to worries about global warming . . . said the newsreader.

"Of course, I don't live in Glenthorn Drive now," went on Daisy after she had welcomed the reassurance that global warming was no more than a recurrent phase in the world's climatic system. "I moved to Hartside Gardens ten years ago. It's a bungalow, better size for me on my own and much easier to run."

After Wimpey's one tiny slip, the listeners remained impressively impassive. Joshua was proud of them.

It was when the local news came on that Daisy thought of the dolls upstairs. She had rested long enough to face another climb.

"I'll be back soon," she said as she stood up. "I'm just going to see the others. They might be pleased to have a visitor."

With that she left the room and closed the door behind her, almost as if an instinct told her to be polite and allow her new guests time to talk alone.

As soon as the door shut, Wimpey turned to look at her mother.

"Does she know?" she asked in a scared whisper.

"Hush!" said Joshua.

Pilbeam squeezed Appleby's hand to warn her not to speak.

Appleby pulled her hand away and looked haughty. What do you think I am, the look said, totally stupid?

The footsteps went clumsily up the second staircase. As they died away, Vinetta turned to the others and said in low, urgent tones, "Whatever we do, whatever we suspect, we must not be lulled into giving ourselves away. You almost did, Wimpey. When you looked up at that cactus plant my heart was in my mouth!"

On the floor above, a door opened and closed quite loudly.

"But what do you make of her?" asked Pilbeam in the same low tones. "She talks as if we could hear."

"We can hear," said Wimpey. "We've always been able to hear."

"But she doesn't know that," said Appleby. "She's pretending. We're not the only ones who have pretends."

"She talks to us," insisted Wimpey.

"She probably has long conversations with her cat," said Appleby. "She's some sort of nutter."

Vinetta looked annoyed.

"We can do without cruel snap judgments," she said. "Let's just wait and see."

Upstairs, the door opened and closed again. Then another door could be heard opening, indicating that Daisy had gone into the next room.

"Poopie talks to Paddy Black," said Wimpey thoughtfully. "Nobody says Poopie's a nutter."

That was true enough. Nobody would *dare* call Poopie a nutter!

"Exactly," said Vinetta, agreeing with Wimpey.

But she was more interested in what was going on upstairs. "I think she must have gone to see Poopie," she said. "We must be ready to go stiff and silent as soon as we hear her feet on the stairs. I hope the others are managing. It's not easy, is it?"

When the feet descended the stairs again their owner did not stop at the living room door. She passed by and went into the nursery.

Poor Hortensia, thought Vinetta. She'll be petrified!

CHAPTER 17

Puzzles

When Daisy closed the living-room door behind her, she stood still for a few seconds in the hall and took a very deep breath.

That doll moved its head, she thought. The doll I call Miranda moved its head to look up at the telly. Daisy's scalp prickled at the thought of what that might mean. Then she pulled herself up sharp and set her reason to work.

For the doll to move her head, deliberately move her head, was clearly impossible. It must have been an accident, a freak movement like the pen that appears to roll off the table of its own accord, or the plastic carrier bag that suddenly collapses because gravity has been operating very slowly. That must be it.

If it weren't for Billy, thought Daisy, I wouldn't have given it a second thought.

Billy Maughan was Daisy's great-nephew. He had seen the dolls in the flat and had been delighted and amazed. It put him in mind of a mysterious adventure he had taken part in three years before. He had been ten at the time. He and some older friends had taken a life-sized blue doll from a deserted country house, meaning to use it for a guy on their bonfire. What happened next had terrified and bewildered them. The doll came to life and made its escape. Billy had told Daisy the whole of this story, but made her promise to tell no one. His parents certainly had no suspicion of their son's nocturnal adventures!

"I imagined it," murmured Daisy to herself as she tackled the staircase, not using her stick but keeping it crooked over her arm, ready for support when she reached the landing. For the staircase itself she relied on the help of the bannister.

"It's easy to imagine things," she said.

But she tapped quite loudly at the door of the big front bedroom, and this time it was not just part of the game, it was a precaution. Of course the dolls *weren't* alive . . . they couldn't be.

Daisy opened the bedroom door and went in. 'Granny' was there, sitting in her armchair with her knitting, 'Grandad' was propped up in bed with his book. Daisy nodded to both of them and smiled.

"I hope you're comfortable," she said. "It may not be what you're used to, but it is a pleasant flat. I've always loved the view from this window."

She went across and looked out briefly at the bridges and the river.

Then, turning her gaze to the room again, she noticed Sir Magnus's purple foot dangling from the counterpane. That was surely not as she had left it?

Must have slipped out, she thought, carefully controlling her active imagination. She lifted the foot and tucked it back into bed. Its owner only just resisted the temptation to thrust it out again!

Daisy sat on the stool by the dressing table and gave Tulip a friendly smile.

"I hope you enjoy knitting," she said. "You look like a knitter. I'm sorry my effort to provide you with the right 'props' is not very good. Knitting was never one of my strong points. Machinery is more my going! I would have made a good mechanic!"

She turned to the doll in the bed.

"My eyes are not what they used to be," she said, "but you look as if you're managing quite well. That book came from Brocklehurst Grove, you know. There was a whole bookcase full of them. All about the Civil War. Funny that. You would never think there was so much to tell. The only thing I remember about it is the story of Charles the First being beheaded in 1649 and it being a cold morning in January. It was a lovely history lesson, that. I always liked history."

Sir Magnus did not move his head. And button eyes do not swivel as human eyes do. But something about him registered alertness. He could almost love Daisy for remembering the king who wore two shirts at his execution lest he should shiver and be thought afraid.

"I would take you both downstairs," said Daisy, "for a change of scene, but I don't think I could manage it. When young Billy comes again, we'll see what we can do. I'm thinking seriously about having a chair-lift put on the stairs. It would be easier for me, and you could both ride down to join us all for dinner."

It was Tulip's turn to be mystified. She sat outwardly impassive in her armchair, but her brain was working in top gear. What does she know, this woman? Why does she talk to us this way? You'd think she knew we could hear her. She should really assume that we can't. She is playing a game, thought Tulip. That must be it. She's playing a game with us, as if we were nothing but . . . and Tulip stopped short as she realised that her thoughts were tying themselves in knots!

"You're very dainty," said Daisy to Tulip, turning her full attention on the little woman in the armchair. "I always wanted to be dainty. But I'm what they call an endomorph. You would be classed as an ectomorph. Lovely words. But in plain English, you're nice and thin, and I am fat."

Tulip was mollified by these words. She liked being neat and presenting a trim figure. Even a rag doll can be susceptible to flattery. A pleasant woman, thought Tulip. A bit odd, but undeniably pleasant.

"Now I'm off to see the boy in the next room," said Daisy. "Then it's down those stairs again to look in on Nanny and the baby. I've a taxi ordered for eight-thirty. I always go home by taxi, have done for years now. I'll look in again on Wednesday afternoon – it's half-day closing. I won't be able to manage tomorrow – too much to see to at home. Good night, now, and take care."

Daisy left the room and shut the door quite loudly behind her.

I felt as if he was listening, thought Daisy, when I mentioned the history lesson . . . but there she stopped herself. I must stop being so fanciful!

So she deliberately turned away from the floppy-eared rabbit in the corner of Poopie's room. She admired the training tower, and talked to Poopie about Billy. Not by the shift of an eye did she betray her consciousness of the presence of the rabbit. Her heart beat faster as she thought, that rabbit was downstairs in the baby's playpen. I'm sure it was. But I suppose I could be wrong. Or there could be two of them.

These thoughts occupied her mind until she reached the nursery.

Miss Quigley looked up as the door began to open and then had no time look down again. She knew, only too well she knew, that she must remain completely still. Googles had already been told to play dead.

Daisy came in, stood with one hand on the doorknob and looked around the room with a glance that was as casual as she could make it. *There was no rabbit in the playpen.*

"I could have sworn there was a rabbit in that playpen," she said, looking directly at Miss Quigley who appeared to be looking directly back. "But I must be mistaken. I've usually found there's a rational explanation for most things that seem strange."

She sat down in the fireside chair opposite the nanny's.

"There was a time when we lived in Glenthorn Drive," she said, being firm with herself. "My mam and dad had gone to the pictures. I got home first to an empty house. We had this bay window with curtains drawn across the front instead of round the inside. I went in and saw the toes of a pair of boots peeping from under the curtains. To be honest, I knew straightaway that they weren't very big or I might have been more frightened. But I did think the house had been broken into and that some youngster was hiding there. I took the poker from the hearth and prodded the curtain. There was nobody there!"

Daisy laughed.

"It was just a pair of boots belonging to our Tommy!"

She got up and went to the cupboard where she had put a baby's bottle, another item brought from the house she had emptied.

"There," she said as she carefully fixed the bottle in Miss Quigley's hand, folding her fingers around it. "You can give the baby her feed."

Then she lifted the stiff little doll from the playpen. Googles was perfect. Not by a flicker or a twitch did she betray the fact that there was life in her.

Daisy placed the baby in the nanny's arms and put the teat of the bottle to her lips.

Poor Miss Quigley! If rag dolls had been liable to sweat she would have been oozing perspiration!

Don't suck the bottle, she prayed.

It is not time to wake up. I am *not* cuddling you, she thought earnestly as if trying to reach Googles by telepathy. You must not move. You must not move.

And Googles, bless her, remained totally inert.

"Is that the time already?" said Daisy looking down at her watch. "Quarter past eight! I'll just pop next door before my taxi comes. I wish I could stay longer! My little house in Hartside Gardens is comfy enough, but it's not the same as being here with you."

Hortensia remembered the old days when the hall cupboard at Brocklehurst Grove had been her 'little house' in Trevethick Street. Is Hartside Gardens a cupboard? she thought. And love, that wonderful drifting feeling that moves about like magic, passed from the nanny to the shopkeeper with a warmth that could be felt in the room. Daisy, on her feet and ready to go, looked down at the baby and smiled.

"I'm going now," she said. "Take care."

She looked in at the living-room.

"Goodbye, everyone," she said. "I won't be seeing you till Wednesday afternoon. So you'll have the place all to yourselves!"

By the time Daisy Maughan had shut the front door behind her and gone off in her taxi, the Mennyms were sure of just one thing. The woman whose house they now lived in was someone they could learn to love.

But to trust? To trust with their secret?

That was something else!

CHAPTER 18

News for Daisy

Daisy was sitting at home in Hartside Gardens on Tuesday evening, accounts all done, books all balanced, not to mention a pile of ironing all neatly pressed. The cleaning lady, Mrs Cooper, did most of Daisy's housework, coming in twice a week, but on Tuesdays Daisy fended for herself. She was just about to watch the nine o'clock news when the telephone rang.

"Hello?" said Daisy and waited for the caller to identify himself.

"It's Albert, Albert Pond," said the voice on the other end of the line. "I hope you don't mind me ringing you this late. I have been meaning to get on to you since Saturday, only I've been very busy."

"I know what you mean," said Daisy. "Too many things happening all at once." She leant forward and switched off the television set. "How is everything? Has Jennifer made any decision about moving yet?"

"That's what I want to talk to you about – indirectly. We still don't know what she intends to do, but Lorna and I have a bit of a problem. Did you know there's an attic at Brocklehurst Grove?"

"An attic?" said Daisy. There would be a loft under the

roof, naturally, but Daisy hadn't realised that there was a room up there. "A room?"

"I don't know how we missed it," said Albert. "There's a staircase leading to it at the end of the top floor landing. It is tucked away and . . ."

Daisy laughed as she remembered the day they looked over the house together.

"And I was so interested in the doll-room that we got no further. My people were meticulous in clearing everything out. But they never mentioned an attic. I suppose since the attic wasn't on any of the lists they wouldn't concern themselves with it . . ."

"That makes sense," said Albert. "The stairs don't look as if they have ever been carpeted, so even the carpet wouldn't have led them there."

"So what did you find in the attic?" asked Daisy. "More things to clear out?"

"A fair bit more," said Albert, "but that's not the problem. I could have cleared most of it myself."

"So what is the problem?" asked Daisy.

"The doll," said Albert.

"Yes?" said Daisy, already feeling apprehensive.

"There's a life-sized rag doll up there, sitting in a rocking chair," said Albert. "It's just like the others, except that it's blue all over, hands, face and everything. But Lorna thought and I thought that it should be put with the others. So if you can send someone over to see to it, we really would be very grateful."

At the other end of the phone there was silence, the silence of someone stunned by the news. Another rag doll! A BLUE rag doll! Thoughts flipped over in Daisy's mind . . . Billy and the blue doll, the purple foot, the rabbit, the head that moved . . .

"Daisy," said Albert. "Can you hear me?"

"Yes," said Daisy. "Yes. I'm just thinking."

She did not want to say anything about Billy. It was much too complicated. And at that moment a convenient thought came to mind. "What about the keys?" she said. "I handed them back. We won't be able to get in."

"I have to go to Manchester tomorrow," said Albert. "I was going to suggest bringing you the keys this weekend, but I have business in Castledean on Thursday afternoon. I could drop them off then if you like."

"That'll be fine," said Daisy. "I could probably have the attic cleared on Friday. No point in waiting longer."

"I'll just be able to pop in for a minute," said Albert, remembering Daisy's hospitality. "It really will be no more than a flying visit. Round about four o'clock, if that's all right."

When she put the phone down, Daisy sat back, thinking of what his words could mean. *There was a blue rag doll in the attic at Number 5 Brocklehurst Grove.* Billy had seen a blue rag doll come to life far away in Allenbridge. Outside a country house there he had seen a girl doll skipping who he was sure looked exactly like the doll now called Miranda.

"I don't know what to make of it," she said. "I just don't know what to make of it."

But she knew how she felt. She felt afraid and over-awed.

On that same Tuesday, just after ten-thirty, Soobie came to visit his family again. They talked deep into the night, speculating on what might happen next.

In the early hours of Wednesday morning, Vinetta saw Soobie to the door.

"See you tonight," said Soobie.

He paused on the front step to fix his goggles in place and pull his hood down over his head. This was the third time he had jogged there from Brocklehurst Grove and returned to the attic at daybreak.

"I'll be glad when you live here officially," said Vinetta.

"It shouldn't be long," said Soobie. "If Albert gives Daisy the keys on Saturday, as he said he would when I heard him and his wife talking about it in the attic, then perhaps I'll be brought here this weekend."

Vinetta looked concerned.

"Will you hate it, being carried as if you weren't alive? Will you manage to play dead?"

Soobie smiled, one hand on his mother's shoulder.

"If Googles can manage it," he said, "I think I can."

He felt fully in control of the situation. He had no way of knowing that Albert had changed his plans, bringing forward by two days his visit to Daisy's shop.

CHAPTER 19

Early Closing

At one-fifteen on Wednesday afternoon Daisy put on her coat and walked along to Number 39. She rang the doorbell very firmly three times before opening the door, as if she were warning a colony of mice to scuttle back to their holes. Shutting the door behind her, she shouted up the stairs, "Hello there. Don't worry. It's only me, Daisy. Early closing today. I promised I'd come and see you all."

When she went into the living-room the Mennyms immediately detected a difference. Daisy did not smile and she did not look directly at any of the dolls. In her nervousness, she went straight to the window and looked out at the river and the street below.

"I think we might be due for some rain," she said. "The sky looks heavy."

She paused, almost as if she thought someone behind her might speak.

Then she began to cling to doubt as others cling to faith. There was no proof that the dolls were living, no proof at all. It was most improbable that they were.

"Not improbable," said Daisy out loud, turning round to look at the dolls, "impossible. Till I see one of you move or hear one of you speak, I won't believe it."

The dolls heard her and understood. Now being stiff and still was not simply for their own protection. It was collaboration with a friendly alien.

Daisy sat down on a dining chair at the table, resting one elbow on the cloth.

"I heard strange news today," she said looking at Vinetta and becoming more easy as she saw that the doll remained motionless. "There is another doll in the attic at Brocklehurst Grove. I haven't seen it yet but I'm told it's blue all over. But it will have a home here, same as the rest of you, for however long it may need one."

Daisy was suddenly aware of what she had said. And what she had said was odd. It sounded as if she were giving them merely temporary accommodation, as if she expected them some day to move on of their own accord!

"Let's have a game of cards," she said, quickly changing the subject. Playing with the dolls was part of her original plan. Following out the plan was a way of holding on to disbelief.

She placed each of the dolls at chairs around the table. It was not all that difficult for her to do. Her legs lacked mobility, but her shoulders were powerful and her arms were strong.

The dolls for their part behaved exactly as any doll should. They flopped forward, they sagged backwards, and they resisted the inclination to giggle at themselves and at each other.

When Daisy had them all seated, she took her own place, between Appleby and Wimpey, and dealt out cards for a game of Snap. Then she took a card from each one in turn, placing them upwards on the table. Whoever laid a matching card on top of one below claimed the whole pile.

The dolls sat stiller than ever human beings could. They ceased to breathe. Breath supplied freshness to their fibre and sound to their voices, but they had no circulatory system making urgent demands for oxyen. To suspend breathing was for them much easier than for humankind.

Of course, Daisy herself had to call "Snap" for them each time. It is the simplest of card games, but everyone sitting at that table was interested in the outcome, even Joshua. Daisy wondered which doll would win. Appleby thought that she was sure to be the winner. Pilbeam wanted Wimpey to win and Vinetta did not care so long as everyone was happy.

The first game was won by Joshua.

"Shall we have another hand?" said Daisy, shuffling the cards and dealing them out without waiting for an answer.

Joshua won again.

"Aren't you lucky?" said Daisy. Then she looked round at the others.

"We'll play something else next time. Perhaps we'll have a different winner."

She put the cards into their packet and put all of the dolls back where they were before.

"I'm going to see the others now," she said. "My taxi's ordered for half-past three. If I don't look in on you again, don't worry. I'll be running short of time."

She went out and shut the door behind her.

In the nursery she was startled to see Googles sitting in the corner of the playpen. Miss Quigley had become confused as to who was where. Since Daisy's last visit she had fed the baby several times and put her bottle away in the cupboard. She had burped her, sung quietly to her and 'changed' her nappy by removing the one she was wearing, refolding it and replacing it as if it were fresh and clean. With all these duties carried out faithfully, it is not surprising that she forgot that Daisy had left her feeding the baby and might expect to find her still doing so.

"My memory's failing me," said Daisy very deliberately.

"I could have sworn I left you nursing the baby!" Then she reminded herself once more of the time she'd seen the boots under the curtain at Glenthorn Drive.

Outside the taxi-driver gave a bleep on his horn.

Daisy looked at her watch.

"Oh dear," she said, "I really have run out of time! I shouldn't have spent so long in the room next door."

So the dolls upstairs were spared a visit. Daisy went off without giving the family one important bit of news. Ted and Michael would be bringing the other rag doll to join them on *Friday* . . .

Soobie visited North Shore Road again on Wednesday evening. Shortly after he arrived it began to drizzle and, though it did not look like coming to much, Vinetta persuaded him to stay the night.

"You can go back to the Grove tomorrow night," she said. "There's no need to go out and get damp."

Joshua was not so sure, but his objections were over-ruled.

"What if Daisy comes to see us tomorrow after the shop closes? She didn't say she wouldn't."

"Soobie can hide in Granpa's wardrobe," said Vinetta. "He can go in there at five o'clock and come out again when we see Daisy leave in her taxi."

Already their landlady, for such they now felt she was, had become too familiar for them to regard her as a stranger, or to refer to her other than by her own name.

CHAPTER 20

Thursday

At ten-to-five on Thursday afternoon the doorbell rang three times.

Upstairs there was consternation. Everyone scattered to their appointed places. Miss Quigley had been sitting at the table with Vinetta, who was holding the baby. Googles was passed over to the nanny who ran out of the living room door and back into the nursery – playpen . . . *play dead!* . . . phew!

Appleby and Pilbeam came hastily out of their bedroom and hurtled past Poopie who was on his way upstairs. Wimpey sat herself down on the floor in front of the television. Joshua was already in his seat. Vinetta went to hers, only to find it occupied by a bewildered Soobie who had had no training in this emergency procedure.

"Soobie!" said Vinetta in a hoarse whisper. "You're supposed to be upstairs in the wardrobe!"

The door below opened and closed.

"Hello," Daisy called up the narrow staircase. "I'm just popping in for a short visit."

Vinetta looked desperately around the living room. The door was closed, as it was meant to be. Soobie was standing in the middle of the room looking large but helpless.

"No time now!" said Vinetta. "What shall we do?"

Step . . . clump. Step . . . clump. Step . . . clump. Step . . . clump . . .
Slowly, inexorably, Daisy was ascending the stairs. To reach the wardrobe on the floor above was out of the question. To go out on to the landing was to invite discovery.

"Quick!" said Vinetta to Soobie. "Get into the cupboard!"

There was a cupboard to the right of the fireplace, a long narrow cupboard whose height inside was reduced by the presence of two shelves. It was not even very deep. Soobie pushed himself in and sat down with his knees up to his chin. Vinetta had to put all her weight against the door to close it. To lower the tiny catch into position was a desperate effort, but she managed it. The task had been made harder by the wedge of blue cloth that had got stuck between the door and the jamb. Inside the cupboard, Soobie tugged at the bit of his sleeve that had become entrapped but it was gripped too tightly to be released.

Vinetta got back to her own seat just in time. There was a tap at the living room door, a polite pause, and then Daisy was standing in the doorway looking in at them all. She was wearing her outdoor coat as usual, but it was fastened up to the chin in a way that suggested that this might not be too long a visit.

"Those stairs don't get any easier!" she said to Vinetta. "I really must see about a lift!"

She came in and sat down on her usual dining chair to get her breath back before going on to explain the main reason for this visit.

"I was just ordering my taxi," she said, "when I remembered I had news that I hadn't told you. Remember what I said about the blue doll?"

She paused and looked round at them before going on. It was then that she saw the piece of blue cloth protruding from the cupboard door. That was puzzling. She knew the cupboard was almost empty. A good shopkeeper always knows where there is spare storage space. I can't remember putting anything in there, she thought. She walked towards the door. The dolls, secretly watching her, held themselves alert. Vinetta knew what was going to happen next, but could not imagine what Daisy would think, or do, when she opened the door.

Then . . .

THUD!

Daisy stopped in her tracks. She turned round apprehensively to see what had caused the noise in the room behind her.

There, doubled up on the floor, was the red-headed teenage doll. Appleby had deliberately fallen forward from her chair just after Daisy passed her. It was a desperate effort, a last ditch attempt to avert discovery.

For a few seconds, Daisy looked down at the doll on the floor and felt a spasm of fear. But the doll had not moved as a person moves. She had fallen awkwardly, accidentally, into a crumpled heap. I must have caught her somehow as I passed, thought Daisy. That's it, she thought, my elbow must have bumped against her.

"Sorry," said Daisy as she raised the doll and placed her back in her seat, gripping her firmly by the shoulders. "Did I catch your arm? That was very clumsy of me."

She was arranging Appleby's hands neatly on the arms of the chair when another noise reached her. From the shop below came the rattle of shutters being set in place. A second later a car drew up and the driver tootled the horn. The cupboard was forgotten.

"There's my taxi," said Daisy, looking towards Vinetta again. "I'll have to be going. Anyway, tomorrow's the day when it will all be happening. Ted and Michael are bringing the other doll – and the rest of the stuff from Brocklehurst Grove – over here at lunch-time. So I'll see you all then."

Daisy hurried out as fast as she could. As the lower door closed behind her, Joshua turned to Appleby and said, "Nice work. Risky – but effective!"

"Diversionary tactics," said Appleby sweetly. "Just diversionary tactics."

Wimpey rushed upstairs to give the others the news.

"Granny, Granny," she said breathlessly, "did you hear? They're bringing Soobie here tomorrow. But he's here already!"

"He shouldn't have been here at all," grumbled Granpa. "He should have stayed where he was. There could be someone in Brocklehurst Grove now, looking for the blue doll and finding out that it isn't there!"

Two hours later, Soobie was sitting in the living-room downstairs, as were all of the family with the exception of Sir Magnus. Even Miss Quigley had joined them and Googles was once more sitting on Vinetta's knee. Soobie could not make the return journey till much later at night, but it was not a worry. The worst, they all thought, was over.

"I was petrified when she saw your sleeve trapped in the cupboard door," said Vinetta. "If Appleby hadn't fallen, goodness knows what would have happened! We can only hope that Daisy won't remember it. She'll have plenty of other things on her mind. I'll be very glad when tomorrow's over though!"

"Tomorrow will be another step forward," said Tulip with determined optimism. "Once Soobie is finished with Brocklehurst Grove, that will be the end of it for all of us. We will be in a position to map out the future."

"What do you mean?" said Appleby, looking with interest at her grandmother.

"It will take some time," said Tulip. "I can't do everything overnight. But we won't be staying here forever. We need a place we can really call our own."

The words left the others speechless. What did she mean?

Before anything else could be said, however, another, more urgent matter forced itself on their attention. A flash of blue lightning lit up the room. There was a brattle of thunder right overhead, followed rapidly by another one even louder than the first.

Then, with the same suddenness, rain began to lash the windowpanes. The drizzle of the night before was nothing compared to this. It was a deluge.

Vinetta hurried to the window and quailed as she saw huge raindrops bouncing up off the pavement. Twisting streams of water were soon overflowing the gutters. Vinetta drew the curtains and Pilbeam switched on the light.

"I hope it eases up soon," said Vinetta looking anxiously at Soobie. "There's no way you could go out in that."

"There's no way I can stay here all night," said Soobie. "If it doesn't stop in the next few hours, I'm going to have to brave it. Before morning I must be back in the attic at Brocklehurst Grove."

"You should never have left," said Joshua crossly. "You should never have been here in the first place."

"Well he is here," said Vinetta, "and there's nothing we can do about that."

"The rain might stop in a while," said Pilbeam. "It can't go on like this all night."

But it could and it did.

At four o'clock in the morning, Soobie decided that, no matter what the weather, he would have to set out for the Grove.

"Is there not an umbrella anywhere?" said Miss Quigley. "You'd think there would be. It's the sort of thing people put in hall-stands."

The remark sounded silly, but they all knew what she meant. Among the bric-a-brac in the cupboards, it was quite possible that there could be an old fashioned hall-stand and that an umbrella might have been left in it. So everyone began to search for anything that might protect Soobie from the rain.

"I can't take a coat," he said. "I wouldn't know what to do with it when I got there. And it might be missed."

Eventually, they found a pink parasol behind some furniture in the cupboard next to the kitchen . . .

"Take it," urged Vinetta. "It's not ideal, but it might help. You can put it out of the way in a corner of the attic."

Joshua went down to the door with Soobie. For a few seconds they both stood in the open doorway looking out at the rain. It was less fierce now, but still extremely wet. Soobie looked doubtfully at the pink parasol with its silk fringe.

"I don't think this will be much good," he said, "and I'll feel blooming stupid carrying it."

Joshua understood.

"Leave it with me," he said. "I'll sneak it back into the cupboard. Keep your head down, stay close to the wall and run as fast as you can. I wish there was more I could do. But there isn't."

CHAPTER 21

Friday

By the time Soobie reached the attic at Number 5 Brocklehurst
Grove his tracksuit was wet through. His trainers were damp
and dirty. Even his face that had been hidden in the hood
was streaked with rivulets of rain. He did not know what to
do about it.

There's nothing I *can* do, he thought as he sat down in the
rocking-chair. He switched on the light and decided to leave
it on till morning came. It made him feel less lonely and a
little bit less wet!

When they come to collect me they'll wonder why I'm
wet, he thought.

I might have dried out by then, he thought, but none too
hopefully.

Then a voice in his head said, whatever they think, they
will never suspect the truth. The truth is too incredible.

In the hours that followed he watched his footprints dry
out in the dust and was relieved to see at least one piece of
evidence disappear.

At eleven o'clock in the morning, Ted and Michael came up
to the attic.

"I told you about these stairs the last time we were here,

but you didn't want to know," said Michael to his older partner.

"I didn't want to know," said Ted, "because I didn't need to know. Daisy pays us to do what she asks. If we start questioning we only confuse things. And if we act off our own bat we end up doing unpaid work that might be unwanted."

They went into the attic and looked at the assortment there.

"There's more here than I thought," said Ted. "Still, Daisy did say we were to clear it completely, so that's what we'll do. Doll first."

The rain had stopped but the sky was still overcast and the light in the room was poor. Ted and Michael went over to the rocking-chair. The blue rag doll sitting there, one hand on each arm, looked very dark. It was only when Ted touched it that he realised that the darkness was heightened by the fact that the doll's clothes were wet.

"What on earth . . .?"

He looked up at the rafters, trying to detect a leak. The underside of the roof looked bone dry. The floor beneath the rocking-chair and all around the attic was dry and dusty. The only wet object in the whole room was the blue rag doll.

A mystery, thought Ted, but not my mystery.

Ted and Michael brought up a crate from their van. Then Ted took the doll's shoulders and Michael lifted its feet and they laid it out straight as a corpse in a coffin.

After that the job was simple. They took the crate down to the van, then the rocking-chair, then followed all the other bits and pieces. And the only thing not as dry as dust was the blue rag doll.

Following Daisy's instructions, the men took everything to their warehouse except the rocking-chair and the rag doll. These they carried straight up to the flat, but not before Daisy had rung the bell repeatedly and shouted up the stairs to signal their arrival. Ted and Michael grinned at each other, but said nothing.

"It's drenched," said Daisy as she touched the doll which had been placed in the rocking-chair that now stood by the living-room window. "What have you been doing with it?"

"Nothing," said Ted. "Nothing at all. It was like that when we found it. We've no idea how it came to be that way. The attic was bone dry. There was no sign of water anywhere."

Daisy looked more closely at the doll.

"You'd better remove the tracksuit," she said. "I'll take it home and get it washed and dried."

Soobie was horrified. There he was sitting in the armchair by the window, in full view of his mother, his father and his sisters, in full view of Daisy and two strange men; and they were about to remove his clothing, a thing that had never happened in all his life. No one had ever seen what he wore underneath!

Ted unzipped the neck of the hooded jacket. Then he and Michael pulled it up over his head. Wimpey held back a nervous giggle as she saw Soobie's blue arms and neck emerging from a pale blue 'vest' that was stitched to his body. It looked, because it was, very old and thin.

They then pulled Soobie forward in the chair, put their hands to his waist and tugged at the tracksuit bottoms. It was almost as if the doll were resisting their efforts, it felt so heavy and stiff. But they managed to pull the trousers over his trainers, leaving his blue legs projecting bulbously from a frayed pair of pale blue shorts.

Daisy took the suit in her hands and was mystified to feel the wetness of it – and even more mystified when she looked at the doll's feet. Its trainers were soaken too, and splashed with mud.

"Where can it have been?" she said. "It looks as if it's been out in the rain."

Her eyes searched the room as if trying to find a solution to the problem from the other dolls. Then . . . the *cupboard*. Her gaze fell on the cupboard where she had seen blue cloth protruding. Yesterday, only yesterday, a wad of blue cloth wedged between door and jamb . . .

There was no cloth there now!

Daisy walked uneasily across the room, still holding the tracksuit, and opened the cupboard door. It was empty.

At that moment came a terrifying suspicion.

Daisy looked down at the clothes she was holding, then round the room again, taking in all of the other dolls, one by one. Blue clothes, blue cloth, a wet night and an inexplicably wet doll . . .

The two men stood silently looking at her, waiting for instructions. Ted coughed.

"Well," he said, "is there anything else you want done up here, Daisy?"

"No," said Daisy with an effort. "I'll see to everything else myself. We'll check the other things later. You can go now. I'll see you at the usual time for the shutters. And thank you both. Prompt and thorough as usual . . ."

Left alone with the dolls, Daisy immediately turned her full attention on Soobie. She looked straight at him and his eyes held hers. In them she saw utter misery. The silver buttons glistened with moisture that bore a startling resemblance to tears. Daisy laid her hand on his arm.

"You are not so wet," she said. "The tracksuit gave you good protection, wherever you were. You'll soon dry out in here."

Then, with a sensitivity that grew as she looked at him, she turned the rocking-chair towards the window. Now the other dolls could not see him, and somehow Daisy knew that this was what he wanted. Vinetta, watching, understood and felt warm towards their 'landlady' for being so perceptive.

Daisy looked down at Soobie's feet.

"I'll take your shoes too. They badly need cleaning."

She lowered herself down to the floor in front of the rocking-chair, painstakingly undid the laces of the trainers, then eased them off, heel first. Underneath, Soobie was wearing a pair of knitted blue socks. Daisy felt them.

"Your socks will do," she said. "They're a tiny bit damp at the toes, but they'll soon dry."

Using the window sill for support, she got up again, turned her back on all of the dolls and looked out at the street, as she had done once before.

"I will bring the shoes and the tracksuit back first thing tomorrow morning," she said, "before the shop opens. Please don't frighten me. If, if . . . Oh, if you really are alive, I think I don't want to know. I need time to take it all in. I need time to sort out my ideas."

It was surprising how little was said and done that Friday after Daisy left carrying Soobie's suit and shoes.

For a start, it was clear that Daisy had been right with regard to Soobie. The chair in which he sat had its back to the room and he remained stiff and mute even after the door downstairs closed. The broad back gave out its own signals. No one must look at me. Till my dignity is intact again, you must all pretend that I am not here.

When Vinetta went to the window and raised the sash a few inches to allow the air in to assist with her son's drying, she never so much as glanced his way. It was clear to all of them that Soobie found his present state of undress absolutely mortifying. It was like the worst of all nightmares.

The waves of sympathy that went out to him were strangely various. Vinetta and Joshua felt sorry for his discomfort.

Pilbeam pitied his embarrassment. Wimpey felt almost as embarrassed as he did. But Appleby, for once in her life, felt at one with her brother. If that happened to me, she thought, I would die. Then a flash of memory told her that something of the sort had happened to her once, but how long ago that seemed!

Sometime later, after a silence that settled upon all of them, Wimpey said softly, "Can I go up and see Poopie?"

"Yes," said her mother, "but go quietly."

No one went up to see Granny and Granpa. It was as if all normal commerce had ceased. At three o'clock, Tulip came downstairs of her own accord.

"Not one of you has bothered to come upstairs and let us know what is happening," she said crossly, "but I take it that Soobie is back?"

Her voice sounded out of place in the silence of the room.

Vinetta nodded but said nothing . . .

Tulip took just one fleeting glance at the rocking-chair by the window. Then she understood. With unusual tact, she did not show any further awareness of Soobie's presence. She took a seat at the dining table and remained there saying nothing, hands folded in her lap, for more than an hour. And the other dolls too remained still and silent. That was their dollness, their difference from restless humanity.

"When the shop closes," said Vinetta, breaking the long silence, "I think we should all go straight to bed. Then Soobie can have this room to himself till morning comes."

It was the only reference she made to her son.

When they heard the shutters clattering against the shop windows down below, they were all relieved.

"The taxi's there," said Joshua, glancing out of the window furthest away from the rocking-chair. He saw Daisy leave the shop. Not for an instant did she raise her head to look at the flat above.

"Bed now," said Vinetta, and, although it was barely five-thirty, not one of them demurred.

Vinetta was the last to leave. She closed the window, was about to say a comforting word to Soobie, but then changed her mind. Sometimes even words of comfort are best left unsaid.

CHAPTER 22

Saturday

Very early next morning, the dolls made their way to their proper places – five in the living room, ignoring Soobie who had not moved from his chair, two in the big front bedroom, one in the smallest bedroom and two in the nursery. The beds were made and everything was tidied away. For two hours everyone sat limply waiting for Daisy to arrive. At nine-thirty, the taxi drew up and the 'landlady' came to the door and rang the bell three times.

"I'm on my way up," she called loudly. "I have brought the tracksuit and trainers for the blue doll."

No panic this time, only relief that the waiting was over.

Daisy came in and, without looking directly at any of them, she went to the blue doll in the rocking chair, and began deftly and gently to dress him, like a nurse dressing a patient. She slipped the tracksuit top over his head, raising first one arm, then the other, to put them into the sleeves. The tracksuit bottoms were not so easy. Daisy manoeuvred them over Soobie's feet, but then she had to raise him from the chair to finish pulling them up around his waist. Finally, she sat down on the floor and fitted the blue-socked feet into the well-cleaned trainers.

"There," she said. "That's better."

She got up and went to the window. With her back to everyone, she began to speak.

"I feel love in this room," she said, "and love is not afraid. How can I fear you when I love you all? I have spent a sleepless night just thinking of it all."

She stopped and sighed. The Mennyms looked at her and began to grasp how difficult it was for her. She was a loving, lonely human being, and she was clearly out of her depth. They thought of the fun they'd had playing cards with her and watching television. Even her lugging them from chair to chair had had its comic side. They wished they had not given her reason to be nervous.

"I don't want to know more than I know already," she said. "I think I can cope with believing, but I don't know how I would deal with certainty. If you are truly alive and need to live here, it will be better if we all pretend that I don't know. And, whatever the truth may be, you are my very, very special friends."

She paused to let them consider what she was saying, though she still did not know whether what she had come to believe in the silent hours of the night was really true. All the evidence of the past and of the present gave her the conviction that, whatever it might mean, these dolls were living beings.

"I will go on loving all of you," she said in a careful voice, as if speaking words already rehearsed, "but it will be different. And I know that loving you will mean keeping your secret."

She paused once more to allow them to consider what she had said, but she did not turn to look at them. She listened and hoped they would not speak.

"We can take things slowly, live from one day to the next," she went on. "I will visit you once a week, on Wednesday afternoons, as if I were coming to tea. No one will pry on you. Mrs Cooper, who does my cleaning, will come in on Friday afternoons between two o'clock and three o'clock to sweep and dust. You will not need to concern yourselves with her. She is a practical woman, totally without imagination and interested only in doing her job properly."

In the street below, Ted and Michael were stowing away the shutters. Michael looked up at the window and waved. Daisy returned the greeting.

"If you are people," she went on after the clatter of the shutters stopped, "whatever sort of people, I cannot go on treating you as if you were inanimate. It cannot be a game any more. If I am wrong, and this is all delusion, then so be it. But I don't need to know everything. Just let me keep a little bit of doubt. That is safer for all of us."

She then went upstairs to see the other dolls.

"I won't be disturbing you after all," she said to Sir Magnus, avoiding eye contact but daring to rest one hand gently on his arm, "There will be no chair-lift and I will not submit you to any troublesome movement. This is your home now. It is not a museum or a show-place."

The purple foot, she noticed, was once more protruding from the counterpane. She did nothing about it.

To Miss Quigley she said, "This nursery is yours. You may do whatever you want with it. My visits will be brief. I would not dream of being an intruder."

Hortensia was baffled. The woman who had a little house in Hartside Gardens sounded so like herself in bygone days, but the meaning was unclear.

"I am just going," said Daisy when she returned once more to the living room. "I'll come again on Wednesday, and not before. This flat is yours now, not mine. I ask only that you move at my pace."

Love there still was, and pity too, but the laughter had

gone out of their relationship. She had once likened playing with the dolls to playing with a giant chess set. But what if the chessmen had lives of their own?

Before leaving, Daisy went to the sideboard, took something from her pocket, and left it there.

The dolls did not stir.

"She knows," said Vinetta, as soon as the door downstairs had closed. "She really knows. And she is going to do nothing about it."

"Do we speak to her?" said Pilbeam. "Do we make friends as we did with Albert Pond?"

"I think not," said Joshua. "That is a woman who knows how to stay within bounds. No games, she said, but we will play by her rules all the same."

"She left something on the sideboard," said Appleby. "Did you see?"

Pilbeam went to the sideboard and picked up the 'something'. It was a pair of keys on a key ring. One was a small shiny one, for a Yale lock, the other was large and rather rusty.

"What can they be for?" she said, holding them up.

"A set of keys for this flat!" said Appleby. "She wants us to be able to come and go as we please. The big one must be for the back door. We will be able to use the back entrance. That is brilliant."

The others looked at her, wondering exactly what she meant.

"So?" said Pilbeam.

"It'll be so much easier. The backstairs lead to an enclosed yard with a high gate leading out into the lane. It's not overlooked at all. From our bedroom window all we can see is a derelict warehouse on top of the hill. We will be able to go in and out whenever we want to."

"We'll see," said Vinetta cautiously. "We'll just wait and see."

It was now that Soobie turned his chair to face the room.

Joshua looked at him. He wanted to bring his son into the conversation, to help him over the awkward bit. He put a hand on Soobie's shoulder.

"Well, that's over," he said, without being too specific. "If anyone does decide to go out, they will have to be wary of the weather."

Soobie forced a smile, but said nothing. However long his life should last, the memory of the past twenty-four hours would never leave him.

CHAPTER 23

Wednesdays and Fridays

Every Friday in the months that followed was exactly the same. The first time Mrs Cooper came in to clean the flat she looked briefly at the dolls, but for her they were just like exhibits in a museum. She hoovered carefully round them. Then she sprayed the furniture with polish and conscientiously dusted everything in sight, whether it needed it or not. After that first Friday, the dolls did not merit a second glance. If anything puzzled Mrs Cooper at all, and very little ever did, it was the fact that her job was so easy.

"Once a fortnight would do," she said to Daisy. "That flat's never dirty, but then it's not lived in. I might as well be doing some washing and ironing for you down at Hartside."

"No," said Daisy. "If the work is easy, just be glad."

Of course, the reason why there was so little work to be done must be quite obvious. Vinetta had been well used to keeping the house in Brocklehurst Grove spick and span. Dusting was a daily ritual, and daily rituals are sacred.

On Fridays, all the Mennyms had to do was switch themselves off entirely for the duration of Mrs Cooper's visit. It became a fairly easy operation, even for Googles. Hush, little baby, don't say a word . . .

* * *

The Wednesday visits were more hazardous but much more interesting.

On the very first Wednesday of the new dispensation, Daisy came into the flat, giving fair warning and feeling nervous, but determined to keep her fears under control.

"Well," she said after she had sat down at the dining table, "I don't know what the future holds, but this is the present and I mean to hang on to it."

The Mennyms in the living room remained absolutely still, but they listened to every word. They sat in their customary places in front of the television set. Soobie's rocking-chair had been turned to face the room. It was a cosy, friendly grouping.

After a thoughtful silence, Daisy went on with her monologue.

"I think I had my suspicions from the start. Deep down. Very deep down. It was just too fortunate that all of the clothes in the wardrobes at Brocklehurst Grove were such a good fit for each of you. And the fact that the clothes were there at all was, well, odd, to say the least."

Ten minutes ticked by on the clock before the visitor spoke again. In that time, Daisy looked cautiously round the room and felt more and more at home. This was the home of her childhood, and these dolls, people, dolls, whatever . . . were hers by choice.

"Then there was that story Billy told me about the dolls he had seen at a house in the country," she said at length, giving Soobie a curious sideways look. "Billy was sure that the blue doll was alive. And that was before I even knew that there *was* a blue one."

Soobie felt a shiver down his back when he heard Billy's name and this very clear reference to his adventure at Comus House. Vinetta's fingers involuntarily gripped the arm of her chair, but Daisy appeared not to notice.

"I'll be bringing Billy to see you again some time," said Daisy, "but it won't be for a month or two. They tell me he's taken a Saturday job in a garage shop. So it will be some Wednesday in the school holidays before he can get here. He'll expect to come. He enjoyed it so much the last time. But he's a well-behaved lad. There's no fear of him doing you any harm."

So Billy has been here before, thought the listeners. They had no recollection of him. It must have been before we came back to life, they thought. All except Soobie . . .

Soobie alone had different thoughts about Billy. Though it had all happened more than three years ago, Soobie clearly remembered the soft-hearted boy who had wanted to save him from the bonfire. What will he say when he sees me? thought Soobie . . . What will he do?

As the weeks went by Daisy and the Mennyms became more relaxed with one another. The Mennyms became less afraid of giving themselves away. They were still careful not to overstep what they knew to be the mark, but if a chair was out of place, or if a newspaper was unaccountably left on the table, they did not worry unduly. Daisy for her part deliberately did not comment upon these minor variations. It was never clear to the Mennyms whether she even noticed them. She always sat in the same seat and talked to them, sometimes watching television, sometimes bringing paperwork of her own and doing it at the table. If she needed anything from the store-rooms she would include that task in a Wednesday visit, being careful to let her 'family' know if Michael or Ted was coming up with her.

At times her conversation made the Mennyms feel that she knew that they were not confined to the house. It was sprinkled with news about events outside that Daisy thought they might find interesting.

"They're opening another new restaurant just by the Dean Bridge," she said. "This area's going up in the world. Over a hundred years ago it was quite posh, then it took a slide into slumminess when the wealthy merchants moved away from the centre of the town. Now it's on its way up again."

Then there was the weather. That was always good for a word or two.

"This heat's no good to me," she said one day when late June produced an unusual spell of very hot weather. "I don't like the cold, mind, but when it's too hot it gets too hard to work. I don't suppose it makes much difference to you?"

She looked at them as if expecting an answer which she knew would not come. The pact she had made with the dolls was by now so well-established. Her glances were always to the left or the right of a face. She was careful never to look any of them straight in the eye. She talked to them like an actor talking down a telephone, pausing for replies from a dead line.

It was just such casual conversation that made them all feel easy, but they knew the rules and they abided by them. Never, ever would they startle their new friend by springing to life in front of her! They all knew it was imperative that the line should stay dead.

Daisy always went to the nursery and visited Miss Quigley and Googles. It was as well that she was prepared to turn a blind eye to change. Hortensia very soon stopped worrying about everyone and everything being in the 'right' place. Sometimes it could be a case of hunt-the-baby. Googles might be in her cot, her bath, her playpen, or just frozen in the act of crawling across the floor. "Play dead," her nanny would say as soon as the doorbell rang. Then she would sit herself on the nearest seat, nursing or not nursing the baby.

Daisy found the second flight of stairs very difficult. So visits to the rooms above were less frequent. Nevertheless, Tulip was always back in her chair beside her husband's bed before midday on Wednesdays, whatever she might be doing the rest of the week. Sir Magnus had no need to prepare for the visitor. He still remained in bed all day and every day. Soon he ceased to consider Daisy at all. She rarely saw him, and when she did it was for only a very short time.

Poopie knew that he had to be found sitting with his back to his bed, 'playing' with his soldiers. Sometimes he had to sprint to his room at the last minute.

And love grew. Only Daisy's regard for the rules she had made kept her from visiting more frequently. In time, these Wednesdays came to be the highlight of her week, the happiest days in her life.

It was by no means a one-sided business. The Mennyms began to look forward to Wednesdays, despite, or perhaps because of, plans they had that would one day bring an end to this routine. They soon learned to return Daisy's love.

"She's a good woman," said Joshua.

"And a clever one," said Vinetta who saw how well Daisy dealt with her business papers and who appreciated all the snippets of knowledge embedded in the lightest of conversations.

Appleby looked surprised. She liked Daisy, but it hadn't occurred to her that anyone might think she was clever.

"I don't see what's so clever about talking to us and not wanting us to answer back," she said. "Sometimes I think she's not quite right in the head."

"She's lonely," said Soobie, in a voice full of disapproval, "and she's very gentle. But that's something you wouldn't appreciate."

"She copes," said Vinetta. "She copes with everything in her own way – even us."

"We cope too," said Tulip "We always have and we always will."

CHAPTER 24

The Rest of the Week

The rest of the week was governed by the opening hours of the shop. As soon as Daisy stepped from her taxi, a different set of rules came into play. Every movement had to be well thought out to avoid making any noise that would be heard on the floor below. Voices were kept down. Family squabbles had to be conducted *sotto voce*. Even Appleby in a rage with Poopie had to hiss venom through half-closed lips! It was very, very frustrating.

Sunday became the day of freedom. The younger twins could romp all over the house if they wanted to. Googles could cry and throw things out of her playpen. Doors and drawers could be opened and closed without such extreme care about the noise they might make. Everyone could breathe more easily on Sundays.

And it was on a Sunday that Appleby and Pilbeam first overcame Vinetta's reluctance to allow them to leave the flat.

"It's easy," said Appleby. "We use the back door. That's why she left us the key. We can sneak out, go up the lane and cut through onto the quayside just past the Low Bridge. There are things we need to buy and, thanks to Granny, we have the money to buy them. If it weren't for Granny we would be in a real fix, but she's managed everything brilliantly. We can buy new clothes, new sunglasses, umbrellas, anything. And we can enjoy just walking about in the open air."

Granny Tulip was pleased to have her expertise so fulsomely acknowledged. So she stayed out of the argument, and her silence was taken as consent. Vinetta was swayed by the plea to be allowed to walk about in the open air.

"If you are very cautious," she said, "I suppose there's no harm. Take notice of Pilbeam and mind nobody sees you going out of the back gate or coming in."

"Not much risk of that!" said Appleby. "This place is dead through the week and double dead on Sundays."

They took their hooded anoraks from the wardrobe, and their gloves. It was the second week in June, but the weather was not at all summery. Their autumn clothes would not be especially remarkable. Another week might plunge them into summer, but for now it was weather to wail about, unless you really wanted to wrap up well!

Appleby was right about the sunglasses. They had none. Daisy must either have sold them or they might be part of the jumble still left in Ted Smith's warehouse. So the first trip out was not as easy as it might have been.

"We'll just have to keep our hoods well down," said Appleby. "And my hair nearly covers my eyes anyway. You're always telling me to push it back. I'll go closest to the stall, buy the first pairs of sunglasses I can lay hands on, and it'll be a cinch after that."

When they were ready to go, Vinetta went with them into the kitchen. There was a flight of six lino-covered wooden stairs leading to the outer door. Vinetta went down them, drew back the bolts top and bottom, then turned the key in the lock. Finally, she lifted the latch and the door swung outwards to reveal a dozen stone steps going down to the backyard.

Vinetta stepped back to allow her daughters to pass. It was eleven o'clock in the morning. The backyard was in deep shadow. There were clouds in the sky and the air was chilly.

"At least it's dry," said Vinetta, "but goodness knows for how long."

"We'll buy some umbrellas," said Appleby. "Even if it doesn't rain today, we might need them next time we go out."

The quayside market sprawled out along the riverside, a longer, slimmer version of the town market that Appleby most frequented. It was not the first time the girls had been there. They knew where most of the things they wanted would be sold.

It was noisy and crowded. Hawkers' voices competed for attention. Many of the things being sold were of no interest to the girls at all – fruit and vegetables, crockery and cutlery, pots and pans. What they sought first were the stalls that had a jumble of jewelry and purses and odds and ends. Among these they found the sunglasses, hardly top sellers on a dreary day, but there all the same.

"Off to the south of France then, darling?" said the stall holder as he handed them over. Appleby passed him the money with gloved fingers, hooded head well down, and said in her most sultry tones, "But of course. Where else? Perhaps you would like to join us. There's plenty of room on Daddy's yacht," then giggled as she moved away.

"I wish you would be more careful," said Pilbeam as she took the glasses from her. "That young man might have thought you were flirting with him. He might decide to follow you. Then what would we do?"

"Don't be silly," said Appleby. "Of course he thought I was flirting with him. I *was* flirting with him. But there's nothing he can do about it — he's stuck with minding his stall, isn't he?"

"All right," said Pilbeam, "all right. But don't do it again!"

Pilbeam, feeling reasonably safe now that she was wearing dark glasses, bought a watch from another vendor and put it right by the church clock. It was a quarter to one. They had both done their fair share of buying.

"I think we should go now," she said.

"Already?" said Appleby.

"We've got everything we came for, so I think we should go," insisted Pilbeam.

"We'll be home far too soon," said Appleby.

"There's no such thing as too soon," said Pilbeam. "Too late is what matters. If we are home by a quarter to two, Mum won't have time to get worried. That might not matter to you, but it does matter to me."

"Can we go the long way round?" said Appleby. "Up the Dog Leap Stairs and down the other side? It's better than going straight back to the flat. It's a bit of fun."

A rapid calculation told Pilbeam that this request would not make them late and so she agreed. They ran up winding stone stairs between high grim walls, along a path that skirted the ruined warehouse, and down another steep flight of stairs to the lane behind North Shore Road. By the time they got there, they were laughing and breathless.

"Isn't it wonderful, wonderful, wonderful to go out!" shouted Appleby as they turned for home. "I hate being cooped up in a cage."

At that very moment, as if in cruel mockery of all she had ever said about the uneventfulness of life in North Shore Road, a car turned into the lane at the far end and was driven at speed in their direction. The steering was erratic and the car mounted the narrow pavement and scraped against the yard walls before veering to the other side of the lane. Its klaxon was playing a jarring series of notes like a primitive war-cry.

Appleby looked towards the noise and then stood frozen to the spot, just watching, mesmerised, as the car came closer and closer. She and Pilbeam were on the wrong side of the lane and their back door was not even directly opposite. The steps they had descended were yards away. Behind them was a scrubby grass slope, steep enough to deter efforts to scramble up it.

"Come on! *Come on!*" yelled Pilbeam, grabbing her sister's arm. "Run!"

They made a dash across the lane and managed to get into their own yard just before the car reached them. They stood breathless with their backs against the inside of the gate. Its wooden frame rattled as the 'joy-riders' mounted the pavement again. For a second it seemed as if the gate might cave in. But the car zoomed on past.

Stillness followed, and a surge of relief!

"There's something to be said for cages!" said Pilbeam shakily. In her arms she was clutching a carrier bag and an umbrella. It was all she could do not to drop them.

Appleby took a deep breath and glared at Pilbeam.

"Something," she said tersely, "but not a lot. Don't you dare mention that car to *them*! It was a one-off. But you know what Mum's like. She would think it was going to happen every time we left the house and we'd never get out again."

Pilbeam looked dazed. Reaction had set in, producing a state of shock . . .

"Pull yourself together," said Appleby sharply. "Give me your bag. You can bolt the gate."

She took Pilbeam's shopping and her own and ran up the steps into the house.

Wimpey was in the kitchen waiting eagerly for their return.

"Have you brought anything for me?" she said and was delighted to be given a musical clown.

That was the beginning of a life that was more tolerable. Within strict limitations, it was almost like living at Brocklehurst Grove. It would never be as comfortable or as easy, but gradually they all made the best of things.

Soobie jogged at night as he had always done. Appleby and Pilbeam sneaked down the back stairs even when the shop was open and went into town. Joshua went out after dark. One night he walked as far as Sydenham's and returned disconsolate, never to know what had happened to his job. Vinetta took the younger twins for a walk along the riverside. She also made outings alone, headscarfed and bespectacled, to the shops she knew well.

Miss Quigley could not find the courage to go out yet. It was doubtful whether she ever would. Her confidence had been shaken too many times. She never even ventured upstairs after the conference. Her area was confined to the first floor of the flat. It was, after all, better than living in a cupboard!

Magnus frequently complained of stress, but in his case stress was intensified by boredom. Daisy had provided him with only one book. His own notes, sheaves of them representing forty years of work, had been thrown out with the rubbish, so absolute was his belief that their end had come. Appleby bought him stationery and writing materials, but he had no heart to start anything, not even a crossword puzzle for the *Times*.

As for Granny Tulip, she stayed indoors till she felt the time was ripe, needing to be completely sure of the pattern of every day of every week before she could embark on all the schemes she had in mind. How carefully she listened to everything Daisy said! How earnestly she read the newspapers Joshua brought home each night! Nothing happened in the shop or in the street below that was not recorded for future use.

She knew that the shop never opened before ten o'clock, that the postman came at nine and then again at eleven-thirty, and that the street was usually empty mid-morning and mid-afternoon. She sent for catalogues, ordered whatever she wanted and when goods were delivered she opened the door carefully, standing in its shadow to take them in, reaching out a lace-gloved hand to sign for them. Black lace gloves were clearly eccentric, but – and this was something Tulip knew well – they indicated nothing other than eccentricity.

By the middle of July, she was ready to embark upon a greater, more exciting and more perilous venture. But the theory of the black lace gloves would see her through. Of that she felt quite sure.

CHAPTER 25

Tulip Makes Plans

"She should've gone when she had the chance," said Magnus, his voice full of resentment. The two grandparents were alone in the big front bedroom, Magnus sitting upright in his bed, Tulip seated rigidly on a high-backed chair.

"Who?" said Tulip, glaring at him so stony-faced that her features looked more carved than moulded. "Dare to say who! Just dare!"

Magnus returned the gaze with one just as fierce, but he did not answer. To talk too much of Kate Penshaw was to enter a forbidden zone. In the weeks since their return to life, Magnus had considered how such a thing could happen. He came to the conclusion that the culprit must be Kate herself. If her spirit had truly left them, they would not be under the stress of living again, and of coming to terms with a different set of rules.

Tulip had reached the same conclusion, but she thrived on stress and was simply glad to be alive.

"We're in as bad a mess as ever," said Magnus, "worse if anything."

"Not worse," said Tulip. "Our leaving Brocklehurst Grove was inevitable. That was an ending. Now we are at a real beginning, better even than the first. There is something truly wonderful that we can do now!"

"And what might that be?" said Magnus scornfully.

"I will tell you later — when the wheels are in motion. To tell you anything at the moment is pointless. You are obviously neither ready nor willing to listen to me."

"Hello. Hello? Lady Mennym here. Lady Tulip Mennym. I'd like to speak to Mr Dobb."

It was three o'clock on a sunny afternoon in mid-July. Tulip, hatted and veiled, was in the telephone box on North Shore Road. She had rung the number of their solicitors, Rothwell and Ramshaw. This long-established firm had served Kate Penshaw first and had subsequently been used by the Mennyms on various occasions. For some years their dealings had been with Mr Dobb, the senior clerk and the partnership's oldest and most revered employee.

"Lady Mennym!" said Mr Dobb in a delighted voice when he came to the phone. "How nice to hear from you again! I thought we might, but one is never sure."

"It is a pleasure to speak to you, Mr Dobb," said Tulip warmly, "a real pleasure."

Mr Dobb had known Tulip's voice for so many years that he could have sworn that they must have met face to face at some time in the past.

"What can we do for you?" he said.

"The second part of my letter," said Tulip. "The contingency for putting all our financial arrangements into reverse. To put it briefly, the scheme we planned for simple living, making our way in this world without the trappings of wealth, has not proved satisfactory. It never had my approval in the first place, as you may imagine, but now the whole family has come round to my way of thinking. We are back in this country and we propose to start afresh, using all the resources that remain to us."

"You have no further claim on the house in Brocklehurst Grove," Mr Dobb warned her hastily. "You surrendered that when Sir Magnus and Mr Joshua failed to sign the certificate of tenancy."

"I know that," said Tulip impatiently. "All we require at the moment is that you will, as arranged, retrieve unopened the letters left by me at the bank and at the building societies. I have sent written instructions to them giving your name as temporary trustee with a full mandate to act on my behalf. You will return the letters to me, still unopened, at Number 39 North Shore Road, which is where I am staying at present. The rest of the family are lodged elsewhere till I manage to make proper arrangements for them."

"I see," said Mr Dobb. By this time a junior had been signalled to extract the Mennym letter from its file and the senior clerk had found the place, on page six, where the 'contingency arrangements' began. "And after that . . .?"

"What I shall ask you to do after that is perhaps above and beyond the call of duty, as they say, but everything will be paid for at whatever rate you consider appropriate. The Mennyms never expect to have something for nothing."

Mr Dobb wondered anxiously what might be coming next. He had had some strange clients in his time, but Lady Mennym was one of his dearest eccentrics. Her letter alone had placed her at the top of his list.

"Whatever service we can give," said Mr Dobb. ". . . if it is within our power . . ."

"It will be," said Tulip crisply. "You may find it unusual, but I feel sure it is not impossible and probably not without precedent."

She's being cagey, thought Mr Dobb.

Then the phone went dead.

Tulip was born knowing how to use a public telephone, just as all of the Mennyms were, but she did not realise just how much change the box could swallow in a short time. So she was obliged to go back to the flat for more.

The shop below the flat was open, of course, but Tulip did not have to pass it. She crossed the road from the telephone box, walked along the pavement close to the wall, and let herself into Number 39 with the front door key.

"Well," said Vinetta, "how did it go?"

"It didn't yet," said Tulip wryly, "but it will. I'll have to put more money in the box. Goodness knows what Mr Dobb will be thinking of me!"

On the next visit to the telephone box, Tulip succeeded in outlining to Mr Dobb precisely what help the Mennyms would need in re-establishing themselves. She came away well pleased with herself and content that an important step forward had been made.

Wimpey eyed her grandmother with curiosity. To see Granny Tulip dress up in her outdoor clothes and go to the telephone box was very, very interesting.

"What's happening, Granny?" she said. "What have you been doing?"

"Making plans," said Tulip, drawing her granddaughter down onto her knee. "Making beautiful plans for all of us."

CHAPTER 26

Househunting

"This is more like it," said Appleby as she and Pilbeam went down the back stairs keeping themselves well tucked-in against the high yard wall. She had on her long green sweat shirt that reached almost to her knees, a pair of printed summer trousers, and the purple-framed sunglasses purchased at the stall on the quayside. A large denim bag was slung over her shoulder. Pilbeam, following her, was dressed more soberly but was also equipped with dark glasses that made her eyes less visible. She smiled to herself but said nothing till the yard door was closed behind them and they were setting off along the empty lane.

"What is more like it?" she said as they turned the corner into the street that led up to the town.

"You know what I mean, Pilbeam. Don't be niggly. Things are beginning to happen again. She's sent us to get some papers," said Appleby impatiently. She looked round at the dingy back street which compared so unfavourably with the place she still thought of as home. Sneaking down the back stairs had been fun at first, but now it was merely an irritating reminder of their situation. In shop hours, only Granny Tulip was allowed to use the front door, and that but rarely.

"Granny has asked us to pick up the property papers from

outside the estate agents," said Pilbeam. "That is hardly a mammoth step forward. Looking at houses is a long way from buying one. If you want my opinion, she's in for a shock."

"What do you mean?" said Appleby.

"She has never bought a house before. She probably doesn't know how much they cost."

Appleby's face dropped, but only for a moment.

"Granny Tulip knows everything," she said forcefully. "She says we are going to buy a house as soon as we find one that meets our needs. I believe her even if you don't!"

They hurried on in silence, under the railway bridge, up Deacon Street and into the town centre. At the top end of the High Street they came to three estate agents on one block. Two of them had their *Property Mart* papers in racks outside the door.

The papers were free, but not clearly marked so. The girls looked at the spacious, well-lit shop inside the plate-glass windows – and felt apprehensive.

"Should we go in and ask for one?" said Pilbeam doubtfully.

"You must be joking," said Appleby. "We wouldn't dare go in there. They'd know like a shot that we weren't genuine customers. We're too young. They'd wonder what we were up to and they'd look more closely."

"But Granny wants the papers," said Pilbeam thoughtfully. "I look older than you. Perhaps if I went in and you stayed outside . . ."

"No need," said Appleby. "It would still be very dodgy, and it's just not necessary. You keep watch and I'll nick a couple of the papers. If they really *are* free, it won't even be stealing."

Pilbeam still felt dubious but she loitered in front of

each stand whilst Appleby sneaked in behind her, removed a paper, and slipped it into her shoulder bag.

"I've got 'em," she said in a quiet, conspiratorial voice. "Now let's walk slowly to the next corner as if we weren't in any sort of hurry."

After they had rounded the corner, Appleby said, "Now for home!" and set off at full pelt down the side street. Not that she was afraid of being caught, but she wanted to get back to the flat double-quick and start househunting.

When they reached the top of Deacon Street, Appleby said, "Come on, Pilbeam, I'll race you the rest of the way."

It was a tempting offer. The rest of the way was all downhill and Pilbeam's legs were longer than her sister's! She looked at the long road that swept down towards the river. But no . . .

"Behave yourself, Appleby," she said sharply. "Do you want everyone looking at us?"

They continued to walk fast and were very soon going up the stone steps that led into the kitchen of Number 39. Pilbeam carefully locked the door behind them and when they went into the living room she put the keys back on the sideboard in exactly the spot where Daisy had first left them.

Vinetta and Tulip were anxiously waiting. Tulip was eager to get her hands on the property papers. Vinetta was more concerned that her daughters should be safe home. Neither had realised just how far the girls would have to walk.

"You took your time about it," said Tulip, looking accusingly at Appleby as they entered the room. "I bet you stopped at every shop window."

"What a cheek!" said Appleby, furiously flinging the papers down on the dining table. "You should try walking from here to the High Street and back. We never stopped once. But nothing satisfies you. I told Pilbeam we should run all the way, but she wouldn't hear of it."

"We did hurry, Gran," said Pilbeam, trying to make peace, "and it is quite a long way. Appleby didn't stop to look at a single shop. She even asked me to run down Deacon Street."

Tulip had the grace to feel a little ashamed of her ingratitude but was not about to show it. She picked up the papers and busily spread them out on the dining-table. Soobie left his rocking-chair and came to join the group. The five of them pored over the Property Marts, passing sheets round from one to another, remarking upon how expensive everything was. Poopie and Wimpey were fortunately out of the way, playing upstairs so as to keep their noise at a distance from the shop below . . .

"This seems possible," said Vinetta, looking at the advertisement for a house the other side of town, overlooking the moor. Even the price seemed fairly reasonable. There was a picture of a detached, three storey building standing in a well-wooded garden.

"Let me see," said Tulip adjusting her spectacles.

"Ha!" she said when she'd looked at it. "Do you know what that price is for? Read the small print! One flat! One two-bedroomed flat on the second floor!"

Vinetta was appalled. At that rate, they would never be able to buy anything anywhere.

"We might as well give up," she said as she considered the other prices on the page. "A house the size we want will cost a small fortune."

Tulip looked prim and mysterious at the same time.

"What makes you think that we don't have 'a small fortune', as you put it?"

"You've spent the past forty years making us feel as if the next gas bill might be an insurmountable obstacle," said

Vinetta. "I never believed that, but I did have the idea that we were not the richest people around."

"Well, we are certainly not the poorest," said Tulip. "If you want the honest truth . . ."

"I do," said Vinetta. "I always do."

"As I was saying," said Tulip, "if you want the honest truth, I would say that we can afford the dearest house on this page, but after we'd bought it we would all need to work hard to pay the bills and build up our capital again."

"How would we do that?" said Pilbeam.

"I shall resume providing knitwear for Harrods, of course. And Bloomingdales might still be interested. Your mother will sew. Your father will look for another job. He can even be Santa Claus at Peachum's again if nothing else comes his way."

Appleby gave her grandmother a look of admiration.

"You're great," she said, forgetting her earlier annoyance.

"Not great," said Tulip deprecatingly. "Just determined."

Soobie had said little. Now he made his contribution.

"There's nothing suitable in either of these papers," he said, "no matter what the price. We need space and we need security."

"We'll have both," said Tulip. "I didn't for one minute think that we should find our ideal home at the first attempt. We keep looking. There's sure to be something out there for us to buy."

"Then what?" said Soobie.

"Then I shall have to speak again to Mr Dobb."

CHAPTER 27

Magnus

The search for another house gathered momentum. Agents were asked by telephone to send details of properties to Number 39 North Shore Road. Tulip gave the name of Thompson as sounding unsuspicious and easily confused with half a dozen other names. This slightly worried Vinetta at first, but Tulip had an answer, as she always had for everything.

"It is called 'muddying the waters' I believe," she said. "When we find something we really want, I will ring Mr Dobb and give him full instructions. No direct contact will be made with the agent after that time. We shall buy under our own name, but no one will connect us with this address."

So particulars of numerous houses were seen – and rejected. The Mennyms were looking for the ideal home. It was not going to be easy.

Meantime, in the room upstairs, isolated from this activity, and having not the slightest wish to hear about it, Granpa Mennym nursed a broken heart.

Magnus just could not get used to being alive again. Each morning Tulip brought him his breakfast on a tray but he did no more than pick at the imaginary meal, pushing it around the plate. Sometimes he complained that the eggs were fried too hard or that the toast was cold. Sometimes he thrust the tray away so vigorously that the crockery and the cutlery clattered alarmingly.

Tulip took all of these sulks and tantrums in her stride. She was so understanding that Magnus felt like thumping her at times. And so cheerful . . . and so optimistic. She just stopped short of singing, but he could swear that she was humming under her breath, something like 'Morning has broken . . .'

The rest of the family weren't much better. Even Appleby never saw him without trying to cheer him up, and that was the last thing he wanted!

Magnus had all sorts of problems. His notes on the Civil War, work of decades, were lost beyond recall. All those references, all those shelves full of books. And what was he left with? One solitary book out of a twenty-four volume work published a century ago! That was all he had left. The Civil War was well and truly over. Scholarship had died in a black bin bag on the first day of October nearly a year ago.

"You should try composing a crossword puzzle," said Tulip. "Remember how much you enjoyed being *Magnopere!*"

"Hmmph," said Magnus dully.

What he could not explain, even to himself, was the disappointment of waking up and finding himself unchanged. His love of learning went much deeper than the famous 'pearls of wisdom' he churned out on all occasions. There had been a moment, at the point of 'death', when briefly, oh so briefly, another sort of knowledge seemed to be within his grasp.

"I'd like to talk to Soobie," he said one day, "just the two of us."

Without a murmur, Tulip went to fetch him. It was not an

ideal combination, but her dour grandson was at least taking a positive attitude towards househunting.

"What does he want?" Soobie asked suspiciously, remembering previous tête-a-têtes.

"A change of company, I think," said Tulip. "And I would be much happier if you managed to get him interested in something. I should be ashamed to say it, but I'm sick of the sight of his miserable face. Goodness knows, I've done everything I can to cheer him up!"

Soobie tapped on the bedroom door and when there was no answer he went in and closed the door gently behind him, just in case Magnus had fallen asleep. He looked towards the bed and was surprised to see his grandfather reading. The book bore the title *A Brief History of Time.* (Appleby had bought it for him at the Oxfam shop in Albion Street. He had tried his best not to read it, but old habits are hard to break.)

As soon as Magnus became aware of Soobie's presence, he hastily shut the book and thrust it to one side. With an exaggerated yawn, he looked up at his grandson and waved one arm towards the chair beside the bed.

"Sit down," he said. "No need to say much. A bit of sanity is all I need, the sight of a face that's not always simpering. At least it's better than listening to your grandmother dispensing happiness."

Soobie nodded his sympathy. It was a tricky situation. If he dared to say anything disparaging about Tulip, Magnus would be indignant. If he expressed support for Tulip's optimism there was every chance that Magnus would throw something at him. So Soobie sat down as he was told and nodded.

They sat in near silence for some minutes, Magnus sighing from time to time. His white moustache drooped; his brows beetled; and his black button eyes retreated into crumpled folds of cloth.

At last Soobie could bear it no longer. He had been asked to come and talk to Granpa. So talk!

He picked up the book that Magnus had discarded.

"I've read this," he said. "Some time ago. I bought it from the book club. It might even be the same copy! I suppose the Ponds could have given my books to the charity shop. They certainly didn't send any of them here!"

"Hmmph!" said Magnus.

"It's a good read," said Soobie, with the glimmer of a smile, "but there's nothing in it to explain the likes of us."

"That's the point," said Magnus. "Nothing on this God's earth can explain how *we* are here. If we were just ordinary, lifeless dolls it would be all right. But we think and we go on thinking year after year. Where does it all lead?"

"I don't know, Granpa," said Soobie uncomfortably. "Remember what the poet said – 'concentrate on this Now'. It might not be much, but it's the best we can do."

Magnus turned on his pillow, raised himself on one elbow and looked directly at Soobie.

"I just wish," he said, "that your grandmother wouldn't be so damned cheerful. She's enjoying this. I think she could go on for a thousand years fixing the future. She's incorrigible."

"Has it not occurred to you," said Soobie cautiously, "that Granny might be right? I mean, we've all the time in the world. If we move from here, you can build up a collection of books again. You can restart your studies."

Magnus looked horrified, black button eyes nearly popping out of his head.

"Not the Civil War," he exploded. "I'm sick to death of the Civil War!"

Soobie was amazed. For years and years and years,

the whole family had humoured Granpa as he studied in great depth the events of the mid-seventeenth century, triumphantly correcting the misinterpretations of other great scholars.

"Reading is your life," said Soobie. "I can't see you living without studying *something*. Why not take up another field of interest? Become a physicist."

"I'm too old," said Magnus, but his fingers twitched over the cover of Hawking's book. "You can't teach an old dog new tricks."

"Rubbish!" said Soobie. "That's a story put about by the young to intimidate the old. Besides, you have time on your side in a way that no human ever could. Do an Open University Course, for a start. As far as I can tell, all of the work can be done by post, especially as you are bedridden!"

"Posted to this place?" he said, looking disconsolately round the room. The book nearly slipped from his fingers and he just managed to save it from falling to the floor. "This one book has to be hidden every Wednesday," he went on, "along with the writing paper Appleby brought, and any newspapers that might be lying around. Your grandmother shoves them all into the little gap under the wardrobe, and then she has the devil of a job fishing them out again. It wouldn't work. There wouldn't be enough space to hide any more."

"We will be moving," said Soobie. "Even I believe that. Granny Tulip knows what she's doing. It'll just be a matter of time. When we move you can have as many books as you like."

Magnus was torn. It sounded very attractive, but could he surrender so easily? It seemed somehow a betrayal to turn from despair to hope, as if he were rejecting the truth in favour of a comfortable lie.

"Too damned cheerful," he growled. But the seeds of recovery had been planted.

"You can go now," said Magnus. "I've got some thinking to do. Tell your grandmother to stay downstairs for a couple of hours. I won't be bothering with tea."

"Is he any better?" asked Tulip when Soobie returned to the living room. "If only he'd eat his meals like anybody else, that would help."

Soobie shrugged. All this business of phantom meals seemed more ludicrous than ever in their new surroundings. His own failure to rebel was down to no more than good manners. He didn't answer Tulip directly.

"Granpa asked me to say that he didn't want to be disturbed, and not to take him any tea." he said. "I left him reading,"

"There! What have I just been saying?" said Tulip. "No tea! Then it will be no supper and no breakfast!"

Soobie put one arm round her shoulders. He was taller and much broader than his grandmother.

"He'll come round in time," he said gently. "In a way, he's coming round already. He is reading, though he's reluctant to admit to it. Once we get another house where he can have more and more books, without having to hide them under the wardrobe, he'll come round."

CHAPTER 28

Billy

The bell over the shop door jangled and a sandy-haired boy of about twelve or thirteen came in. Daisy looked up from the cameos she and her customer were handling.

"Excuse me a minute, Mr Lucas," she said. "That's my nephew's son. I'll just have a word with him."

She walked over to Billy and grasped his arm warmly.

"It seems ages since you were here last," she said smiling, and looking delighted to see him. "But now you're just a little bit early. I'll be shutting up shop at twelve. Do you think you could go into the kitchen and start brewing us a pot of tea?"

The kitchen was at the rear of the shop. Billy was partly flattered to be entrusted with tea-making, but it was not what he had expected.

"I could go up and wait in the flat," he said, looking towards the pocket in Daisy's skirt from which, on his last visit, she had produced the key to the house upstairs. For him, Number 39 North Shore Road was magical – and that was without knowing the most wonderful of the dolls' secrets.

"Not this time," said Daisy. "We have things to talk about first. And I've made you some cake and a few sandwiches. We'll eat first and have a look upstairs later."

Billy was disappointed but he went into the kitchen and left Daisy to her work. Last time, she had let him go upstairs on his own to see the dolls. He had moved them about, setting them in new positions. He had played with the soldiers, pretending that the doll in the room above was a real little boy. He had fixed up the playpen in the nursery and put the baby in it. Had he done something wrong?

The customer departed and Daisy shut the door after him, turning the CLOSED sign towards the street. Then she hurried into the back kitchen where the kettle had already boiled and the tea was brewing. From the cupboard above the fridge she took out plates full of food, far more than the two of them could expect to eat, and put them on the table.

"Shall I pour," she said to Billy, "or will you?"

Then she sat back and waited as the boy poured tea into their cups.

"You're looking very grown up," she said. "I'm sure you've grown a lot in the past few months. Or maybe I've shrunk again! People do as they get older, you know."

Daisy laughed, knowing that her shortness of stature was a thing that sometimes made people feel sorry for her. But not Billy! He knew better.

"You always say that," he said, "and I used to believe you. When I was really little, I honestly believed you!"

Daisy gave him a wistful look.

"That's what we'll have to talk about now," she said. "What you and I honestly believe."

Billy gave her a sharp glance. He was a bright boy and he understood immediately that the words held some special meaning.

"It's what we don't know that I'd like to talk about," said Daisy seriously. "What we don't know but might honestly believe. Do you remember that blue doll you told me about?"

"Yes," said Billy slowly, wondering what Daisy was leading up to.

"It moved," said Daisy, "and it even spoke to you once."

"Yes," said Billy ruefully. "It said it would crush me bones. But it didn't mean it."

"How d'you know?" asked Daisy. She leant across the table and looked at him very earnestly making him feel that what he said really mattered.

"I just know," said Billy. "It had a nice face, and it waved goodbye when it left in the man's car the next night."

"And then," said Daisy, "at that point, what did you believe? Did you think it was a trick, or a robot or what?"

Billy struggled to put into words the feeling he so well remembered, the feeling that he and Joe had shared as they crouched behind the wall at Comus House and saw the blue doll wave its arm in their direction. Anything he said would make him vulnerable. But he trusted Aunt Daisy, trusted her even more than he would his own mam and dad.

"It was real," he said.

"What do you mean?" said Daisy, pushing him to say more.

"It was alive, just as if it were human. Leastways, that's what I believed then."

"And now?" said Daisy. "What do you believe now?"

"Same as I believed then," mumbled Billy and he bit vigorously into a cheese scone. "It was living, just like you and me."

Daisy took the cosy off the pot and poured herself another cup of tea.

"Another for you?" she said, nodding to Billy.

"No thanks," said Billy. Eating and drinking had become an interruption. He looked at Daisy expectantly, waiting for what she would say next.

"The dolls in the flat upstairs," began Daisy. "I think that they are living. I haven't seen them move or heard them speak, but I have reasons for believing that they are alive and can hear every word I say to them."

Billy gasped.

"Tell me," he said, "tell me all about them."

So Daisy told him the tale from beginning to end, told it simply and had him believing every word. When he heard about the blue doll, he wanted to go upstairs there and then to see it, but Daisy made him hear the story out, finishing with all the details of the pact she had made with them.

"We won't see them move," she said, "and they won't talk to us."

"So how will I know they're really living?" said Billy.

"You'll know," said Daisy. "You'll know."

"Can we go and see them now?" said Billy. "The blue one must be the one I knew. It couldn't be any other. I mean – how could there be two?"

Daisy got up from her seat and went to take her coat from the coat stand in the shop. Billy followed.

"One more thing," said Daisy as she fastened up her coat. "You won't be able to move them around as if they were just dolls. Think of them as people, talk to them as people, and show them the same sort of respect you would show to any other human being."

When they reached the doorway of Number 39, Daisy put her key in the lock as usual, but at the same time she rang the bell three times emphatically. Billy watched her, wondering.

"We're on our way up," Daisy called up the staircase as they went into the lobby. "I'm bringing Billy to see you. You remember. I told you about Billy."

To Billy, she said, "I'll go first. I know I'm slow, but it's better that way."

CHAPTER 29

Recognition

"They're different."

Billy looked at the dolls in the living-room. His back was towards the blue doll, but even before he saw Soobie he knew that these dolls had changed in a way that was subtle, but recognisable. He touched Vinetta's hand which rested quite limply on the chair arm. Beyond question, she was as still as any statue. No breath passed her silken lips, no tremor stirred in face or fingers.

"They're different," said Billy again. "Last time I was here, they were paler and stiffer, as if they'd been starched. Now they are, I don't know, somehow soft."

Daisy stood in the doorway, measuring his words.

"More alive, do you think?" she said, coming right into the room and standing by Joshua. And now it seemed to her that she had known this from the first, known it and wilfully ignored it. When, all those months ago, the dolls had been delivered, and had been removed so gently from their crates, they had indeed been much less supple and much paler than they were now.

When had it happened?

How had it come about?

'When' was an easier question to answer than 'how'.

"The night Miranda moved her head," said Daisy. "Before then I noticed nothing. I assumed that they were what they were meant to be – a family of rag dolls."

Billy looked at her, wondering. Then his gaze shifted to the doll in the rocking-chair, set a little apart from the others, half-turned towards the window. It was not quite the blue doll he remembered. The tracksuit with its neat white trim was nothing like the tattered striped suit the doll had worn three years ago. But the hands were the same. The head was the same. And the eyes, yes, the eyes were the same. Billy looked at the silver buttons set in the blue cloth face, and saw life.

"Oh!" he said. Then "Oh!", a deep "Oh" coming from the bottom of his heart. He sat down heavily on a dining chair, his right arm coming to rest on the table. His face was drained of colour. Even his lips had whitened, so deep was his state of shock.

"Are you all right?" said Daisy anxiously.

Billy looked at her but said nothing. She sat down on the chair beside him and covered his hand with hers. The large, plump hand gripped the boy's thin fingers, promising safety. Billy looked at Daisy and his eyes brimmed with tears, silly, childish tears that he wiped away vigorously with the hand that was free.

"It's a shock," he said. "I mean – it's a shock. They *are* alive. Really alive. And the blue one is the doll we took from that house near us. I don't just think he is. I *know* he is."

He looked round at them as if he expected them to speak or move. A tension filled the room, waiting to be broken, and there was a moment when . . .

But it passed. The Mennyms remained frozen, united in their resolution to suspend animation. That was the pact.

"They won't move," said Daisy firmly. "They won't talk.

You *believe* that they are alive, but you will never know for sure."

Billy sat dazed for some minutes. Daisy said nothing more. She just sat there beside him and let him take his time. She was relieved to see a more natural colour returning to his cheeks. The worst was over. Then, slowly, Billy stood up and clutching the edge of the table he said in a low voice, "Can we see the others now?"

"Are you sure?" said Daisy, still worried that the ordeal had been too much. I should never have told him, she thought. I should have kept it to myself. But what else could I do? He knew so much already. I couldn't just say they weren't here any more. I couldn't lie. And I couldn't let him come up here without any warning.

Billy walked over to Soobie and put one hand on his shoulder. The chair rocked slightly, making Billy jump. Then he smiled sheepishly as he realised that it was his own movement that had set the chair rocking. He gave Daisy a brave look.

"We'll go to the nursery first," he said. "I want to see the doll in the playpen."

"If she's still there," said Daisy, a faint smile returning to her lips.

"What do you mean?" said Billy.

"She might have been moved," said Daisy. "I can't quite remember where she was last."

Billy lifted Googles out of the high-chair.

"I think I'll put her back in the playpen," he said, looking at Aunt Daisy. "Is that all right?"

He was holding the doll up, one hand under each arm, and he was aware that she too was softer than he remembered and pinker in the face. The curl on her forehead looked springier, not plastered flat against her brow. Daisy nodded approval and Billy sat the doll in the playpen with her back against the corner post. Googles remained rigid but there was a warmth about her that no deliberate rigidity could dispel.

"Now," said Billy, looking round the room, "where's your rabbit?"

"It's upstairs in the boy's room," said Daisy. "I think it fits in better there."

In Poopie's room, Billy saw the rabbit sitting upright on a stool in the corner, and somehow he felt that, no matter how odd the idea seemed at first, Daisy was right. The rabbit, of course, was the same as before, totally inanimate.

Billy looked thoughtfully at the assault course he had set up on his first visit, spending hours turning the whole room into an arena for military manoeuvres. He opened the cupboard door where Poopie's other toys were stored. Something about Poopie's face made Billy sense that the doll would like to play a different game.

"I think I'll put the training tower away and get out the Lego bricks," he said. Daisy had kept the bricks, putting them in a large wooden box, planning for just such an occasion as this. "That's if you don't mind?"

"Go ahead," said Daisy. "I don't mind, and I'm sure he won't! Do you want me to stay with you, or shall I go back to the shop? Either way suits me. I have some paperwork I could be doing."

Billy looked at the boy doll and then at Daisy.

"I'll be all right," he said. "He understands the pact. I think he'd like me to play here. It'll be company for him."

"You're sure you're not . . . afraid?" said Daisy carefully.

"Not now," said Billy slowly. "I was at first – just a bit. But not now."

Poopie watched as Billy carefully put all of the Action Men and their equipment away in boxes in the wardrobe. Then he drew out the monster box full of Lego bricks. The boat

Poopie had once made was not quite intact, but it had not been completely broken up. Its batteries were flat but that didn't matter much. Billy set about restoring it. Then, thrilled with all of the different resources the box offered, he went on building more and still more. The ship paid a visit to a desert island where there were palm trees beside a Lego hut and small boats beached on crystal sands . . .

The afternoon passed too quickly.

"Billy!" called Daisy from the foot of the stairs. "I think you'd better come down now. It's nearly tea-time. Your mam and dad will be here soon."

What she meant was, it was safer for him to be downstairs in the shop before his parents arrived. The secret of the dolls was not for sharing. Jamie and Molly Maughan would not be invited to pay them another visit.

Billy understood.

"See you next week," he said to the doll on the floor. "I'll bring some batteries. You've got everything else."

CHAPTER 30

The Robot

When Billy came the following Wednesday, he and Aunt Daisy parted company on the landing.

"You can play with the doll upstairs. I know that's what you'll be wanting to do!" said Daisy. "I'll stay down here with my friends. Pop in and see the old couple; say hello to them for me."

Daisy was right. Billy was longing to get back to what was for him an Aladdin's Cave full of toys. He liked Poopie, though of course he did not know his name. What is more, among the dolls downstairs was Soobie. And Billy was still wary of the blue one, the doll that seemed to him more magical than all the others.

"I've brought some batteries," said Billy. "I told you I would. I bet you thought I'd forget. I've got three new sets in different sizes. Took them off me wages at the garage."

Poopie looked straight ahead of him at the Lego that was still spread out over the floor after last week's game. This was fun, he thought, a bit scary but fun all the same. And it wasn't easy – to spend two or three hours pretending to be dead.

Billy went to the wardrobe that was full of toys stacked up

in boxes. Methodically, he lifted one box out after another, continuing his investigation of their contents and replacing them carefully after he had finished. Then, right in the corner of the wardrobe, propped up against the back panel, he found the robot. By its side was a matching remote control complete with antenna. Excitedly, Billy slid the cover off the battery case, found batteries stained and clearly dead, but was pleased to note that they matched one of the sets he had brought with him. He even had the larger batteries needed to fill the gaps in the robot's chest.

And there began the game for the day.

It took some time to set up.

He began by lifting a puzzled Poopie onto the bed and settling him with his back against the wall.

"You can watch," he said, "but you mustn't get in the way. That robot needs space."

The Lego bricks had to be boxed up again. The only things Billy kept from last week's effort were some long plastic leaves, spreading out in fronds like jungle vegetation.

"We'll need those," said Billy.

Then he got out half-a-dozen Action Men with rifles, a few plastic bushes and a fence or two. On the floor he spread out crumpled sheeting for yellow sand and some brown cloth to go under the plastic greenery. Finally, he went back to one of the boxes he had already explored and brought out an assortment of lions, tigers and leopards.

"That'll do it," he said.

Poopie sat watching and wondering. He had liked the robot well enough when his dad first bought it for him. But he hadn't played with it much for ages. I mean, what's the use of a toy that doesn't belong to a set and just moves back and forward bumping into things?

Billy tested out the batteries. The robot moved clumpily forward, raising legs that did not bend at the knee.

"That's fine," said Billy.

Then he completed the landscape. Between the wardrobe door, which he left wide-open, and the centre of the room in front of the bed, there was the jungle, all trees and swaying branches with animals stalking. The other half of the room was a desert battlefield with soldiers lying on their stomachs in the sand, hiding behind boulders, taking aim ready to fire.

Billy looked at the scene he had created and was satisfied. He then took the robot to the doorway.

"This is Chang," he said, looking across at Poopie, "Chang the Mysterious, walking the earth in search of his own kind, feeling forever lost and lonely. Persecuted by men and feared by the beasts."

Billy pressed the button and set Chang moving. It was not easy at first. The robot tended to go off in his own direction because the rocking button on the remote control had to be handled very precisely. He went off over to the window and became entangled in the curtains that fell in folds to the floor. Then he made a right turn that was slightly too sharp and he fell over sideways. But eventually Billy got the knack of it and the robot returned to the room door.

Next he set off across the desert. He was twice the height of any of the soldiers, and four times as broad. His metal feet could easily have crushed them. But they were hidden from him. He walked past them, unseeing, at a slow steady pace. They fired at him and he was so large a target that they could not miss but their feeble bullets, even had they been real and not pretend, could make no impact on his powerful frame. He strode off, unharmed, to the edge of the jungle.

There he stood still whilst Billy moved the lions, the tigers and the leopards into hiding, making them scatter to one side and the other, taking refuge in the undergrowth.

"Look!" he said to Poopie. "They're all running away from

him. He wouldn't harm them. He would love them and make pets of them. But they don't know that. So they run off and leave him lonely as ever."

When the beasts had been made, artistically, to flee, Billy set the robot moving again, towards the wardrobe, till he fell into it. He lay there like an injured man. Billy stood him on his feet again and pointed him towards the room. Then the robot walked stiffly but directly to the foot of the bed and stood there looking up at Poopie.

Poopie thought the story wonderful and was dying to say so, but the pact, the silly old pact, kept him in check!

Billy picked up the robot and put it on the bed beside Poopie. Then he tidied the toys away again and closed the door. Poopie's arm was draped around Chang and Billy decided to leave it there.

"Billy!" called Daisy from the floor below. Time we were going now. Taxi'll be here for me in twenty minutes. I'll drop you off at the bus station."

Daisy had spent a peaceful afternoon watching an old black-and-white film on TV, a love story set in a poor quarter of Paris, a seventh heaven in a run-down tenement flat.

Alone in his room, Poopie was free to move again. He looked at the robot sitting stiffly beside him. He thought of the story Billy had told, and he cuddled it to him as if it were as soft and as lovable as a teddy bear.

"You needn't be lonely," he said. "I won't put you back in the cupboard again. You can sit on a cushion beside Paddy Black. He's only a rabbit, but he's good fun."

CHAPTER 31

The Green Rover

"Are you sure you don't mind being left all on your own?"

Daisy opened the front door of Number 39 to let Billy in, but she herself remained out on the pavement. In the roadway, Billy's dad was waiting in the car. This was the last Wednesday of the summer holidays and it was following a different pattern. Daisy was leaving Billy alone in the flat whilst she went shopping with his parents.

"Of course I don't mind. It's much better than traipsing round shops all afternoon," said Billy, turning to wave to the car. "You don't know what you're letting yourself in for!"

As soon as Daisy left, Billy closed the door behind her and set off up the staircase. Under his arm he was carrying a box the size and the shape of a shoe box.

"Aunt Daisy's not coming up today," he called loudly to warn the dolls of his coming just as Daisy always did. "I'm here by meself."

He went into the living room first, looked shyly round and said, "Hello, everybody. I'm just going to play upstairs. I'll be down again when the doorbell rings. They're coming back for me at five o'clock."

Then he turned on the television set, partly hoping to

please the dolls, partly feeling more comfortable with a noise in the background as he turned to go.

He stood for a second in the doorway, glanced furtively at Soobie who was in his usual place in the rocking-chair, opened his mouth to say something else, and then changed his mind. He was used to Poopie now, at home with Poopie, but he still felt just a shade nervous of the big blue doll.

He looked in briefly on Miss Quigley and told her that Daisy wasn't coming today, which news Miss Quigley received as impassively as ever, not showing the disappointment she felt. She had come to welcome Daisy's visits. They gave a pattern to the week.

On reaching the next floor, he did no more than put his head in at the door of the grandparents' room. Then he went to join his playmate, eager to show him what he had brought.

The box lid was taken off to reveal another box inside, a display box in clear perspex with a black base. And in the box was a car. The car . . .

Poopie, seated on the side of his bed where Billy had left him last time, found it hard not to lean forward and look more closely.

"This is the car," said Billy removing it carefully from its stand. "It's a Rover. That colour's called British Racing Green. The seats inside are padded . . ." he opened the front door ". . . the doors open properly, all four of them . . ." his fingers delicately turned the steering wheel ". . . and it really steers. The wheels turn left or right as you turn the driving wheel."

He lifted it up and placed it carefully on Poopie's knee, but without leaving go of it. Poopie was delighted. It was desperately difficult not to show how delighted he was.

"It's not a toy, you know," said Billy. "It's a real scale model. My mam bought it last week. It's what she calls an unbirthday present, because my birthday's right near Christmas and it's the holidays and we haven't been anywhere."

Poopie felt like saying – My birthday's on Christmas Day. They've never thought of giving me an unbirthday present.

He felt like saying – I know what you mean about it not being a toy. Paddy Black's not a toy either.

But, oh, above all, he was itching to get down on his knees and steer the car and push it gently, ever so gently, over the carpet.

Billy took the car from Poopie's hands and put it on the floor. Then, knowing instinctively what his friend wanted, he sat Poopie on the floor beside it. They sat there facing each other with the car in between them, Poopie's back resting against the Lego box that Billy had not put away on his last visit.

"Look, it even has proper mirrors," said Billy, "and a glove compartment that pulls down."

Without standing up, Billy twisted round to pick up the display stand. As he reached out to grasp it, his back was towards the doll. When he turned again he was amazed to see that the car had changed position and was facing the window.

He looked sharply at Poopie. The doll was still as a doll should be, but frozen in a different stance from before, its upper half inclined towards the car.

He's moved, thought Billy. *And the car's moved. He's moved the car.*

He looked into Poopie's face and detected something like fear in the doll's blue eyes, the fear of being found out. And at that point Billy realised that he himself had come far enough not to be afraid, not even if his friend stood up and did a dance in the middle of the room.

He can move, thought Billy, *I know he can move – but can he speak? Will he speak? Can I get him to talk to me?*

"I don't mind if you talk to me," said Billy, looking Poopie straight in the eye. "I wouldn't be frightened. And I wouldn't tell anybody."

Poopie heard the words and was thoroughly alarmed. The pact might be irritating, but it was important. They all said it was important. They had warned him over and over again. So he sat there, his back braced against the box, and he concentrated hard on being a doll, on saying nothing, doing nothing, not even drawing breath.

Daisy had told Billy to treat all of the dolls with respect, but by now Poopie was more person than doll. Billy felt irritated with him for playing the game of stiffness and silence. He raised Poopie's left arm till it pointed to the ceiling. Then he let it go and it dropped leadenly back into place. He did the same with the right arm.

"You're not being fair," he said. "I didn't ask for any pact. The pact was Aunt Daisy's idea, not mine."

But Poopie remained as still and impassive as ever.

"Two can play at that game," said Billy at last. "I'm going to lie on your bed and go to sleep. You can do whatever you want."

He flung himself down on the bed with his head on the pillow, his face turned towards the room. His eyes closed immediately and he took on the look of a peaceful sleeper breathing softly and regularly, arms stretched out and still. Poopie, seated on the floor at the bottom of the bed, had a close-up view of Billy's right foot, or to be precise, the corrugated sole of his training shoe. Focussing as best he could, without moving his head at all, he could see the face on the pillow. The eyes were closed, thick pale lashes fringed the cheek.

And on the floor there was still the beautiful car just begging to be played with.

Poopie sat impatiently waiting for half-an-hour.

Billy began to snore lightly.

Another half-hour passed.

The boy on the bed was what Granpa would call 'out to the world'.

Poopie looked longingly at the car and stretched out one hand to touch it. His palm settled on the shiny roof . . .

"GOTCHA!" cried Billy, jumping up from the bed. "I knew you could move. I just knew you could. And I bet y'can talk as well."

Poopie sprang to his feet and gave Billy a look of terror.

"You cheated," yelled Poopie. "You cheated."

And he ran from the room and down the stairs.

CHAPTER 32

A Different Pact

In the living room below, the dolls sitting round the television set were watching a gardener digging a trench and filling it with some sort of compost. It was not the most scintillating of broadcasts but they had no other choice. The pact demanded that they should not interfere.

Then suddenly from the floor above came the sound of Poopie's voice and the clatter of feet. The Mennyms were filled with consternation.

The feet came running down the staircase.

Soobie looked at the others and then put one finger to his lips.

"You must all keep the pact," he said. "That is best. I will break it and I will do what I can to put things right."

"Why you?" said Appleby.

"He knows me," said Soobie. "I have spoken to him before. And if we all came to life in front of him, just think how frightened he might be. In this flat, at this moment, he is outnumbered."

Soobie's voice carried authority. There was no time to argue. The others all froze just as the door burst open.

Poopie came into the room, closely followed by Billy. Neither was fully aware of the rest of the Mennyms. Poopie's fear was turning to anger and he was just about ready to turn and fight. Billy was reaching a hand out to grab him as he might a smaller boy in the playground.

"Mind the flex!" shouted Soobie. "Do you want to pull everything over?"

Billy and Poopie stopped dead and looked in amazement at the big blue doll that was standing in front of them.

He's broken the pact, thought Poopie.

I knew it, thought Billy, I knew it, I knew it all along.

Firmly but gently, Soobie placed one hand on Poopie's shoulder and the other on Billy's.

"Calm down, the pair of you," he said. "Take it easy." And, leading them to the dining table, he sat them down on the chairs and drew up another chair to sit beside them. They had their backs to the others in the room. Soobie, at the far side of the table, sat facing. He could see the rest of the family. Over Poopie's head he signalled to Joshua a reminder that they should all keep still. Joshua gave just the ghost of a nod.

"Now," said Soobie, "we'll have to talk."

"It wasn't my fault," said Poopie hastily. "It was his. He tricked me. He . . ."

"That's not important," said Soobie. "What matters now is that Billy here knows everything."

"I can't help that," said Billy. "If you weren't alive, I could never have found out that you were, could I? No trick in the world could bring you to life if you weren't alive already."

Billy and Poopie glared at each other, the older boy ready to slap, the younger one wanting to kick. Even the best of friends can come to blows!

"And that's not important either," said Soobie, feeling like an older brother to both of them. "I'm not interested in blaming either of you. Our problem is what happens next."

Suddenly to all the listeners in the room that seemed a

massive problem, one without any solution at all. They sat for some minutes in silence.

Billy was struggling with all sorts of weird thoughts. What would they do to keep their secret? Were they aliens from another world? Might they even murder him? Daft idea! If they were aliens, they were friendly aliens. He felt quite sure of that.

"What are you?" he said, looking keenly into Soobie's silver button eyes and seeing not a doll but a person there.

"We don't really know the answer to that," said Soobie. "Do you know what you are?"

"That's not a fair question," said Billy. "And it doesn't matter any way. I know that you are alive and you are not made of flesh and blood like me. You don't want me to know that. So what are you going to do?"

Soobie recognised Billy's bravery, his determined facing up to the situation. He had always liked Billy, ever since Comus House.

"You tried to save my life once," said Soobie. "You cared what happened to me. I care what happens to you. But we must have some sort of understanding. Just sit and listen till I tell you the story of the Mennyms. Then we will talk about what happens next."

They listened in silence as Soobie went back to the beginning, or at least to the time when they had come to life in the attic at Number 5 Brocklehurst Grove. Sometimes the tale was hard to hear without weeping but the dolls in the room showed no sign that the suffering had been part of their lives. They kept the pact as rigidly as ever.

"And now," Soobie ended, "we are looking for another place to live, a place where we can be ourselves and have no fear of being found out again."

"You can stay here. I would never tell on you," said Billy. "Never ever."

He looked round earnestly at all of them but apart from Soobie and Poopie there was no other evidence of life in the room. But there was warmth there. Billy wanted to talk to all of them, to hear all of them speak.

"No," said Soobie, reading his thoughts. "They won't talk to you. It is better as it is. After today I shall never speak to you again and never let myself be seen to move. That is how Daisy wants it to be. She has looked after us well and we would not hurt her. Belief is all she can cope with. Certainty might cause her heart to stop."

Billy flushed.

"I wouldn't hurt Aunt Daisy either. She's one of the nicest people I know. But what do I tell her?"

"Tell her nothing," said Soobie. "Let this afternoon exist in a bubble, a place all of its own."

"Like UFOs," said Billy catching on to the idea.

"A bit like that," said Soobie with a smile.

"But what about next time I come?" said Billy. "Daisy'll be here, but can I not mebbe just talk to Poopie upstairs when we're playing? And let him talk to me."

Soobie gave it thought and decided that such an arrangement wouldn't hold for long.

"Please," said Poopie as he saw his brother ready to say no. "He's my friend. I've never had a friend like him before."

"It won't be till Christmas anyway," said Billy, thinking the time interval might turn the balance. "I'm back at school next week."

His words gave Soobie a feeling of relief.

"Christmas is a fair way off," he said. "What is it Granpa says? – A lot of water will have passed under Dean Bridge before then. So perhaps we should just wait and see."

Then Soobie went with them to the room upstairs, to take

the strain off the rest of the family. The door bell should ring in less than an hour. The ordeal would soon be over.

For Billy and Poopie it was no longer an ordeal. They were friends again. They showed Soobie the car, and then Poopie brought the robot from its cushion.

"He's called Chang," said Poopie, "and Billy made up a lovely story about him. Now he sits beside Paddy Black so he won't be lonely."

Soobie smiled and wondered how one measured loneliness.

"And when you go to your new house," Billy asked him as they sat comfortably together, "will you live there forever, never getting any older, always being just as you are now?"

"Yes," said Soobie. "I suppose so."

"But that means you will never really die. That's wonderful. We hated it when my grandad died."

"I'm not so sure how wonderful it is," said Soobie. "What about the Wandering Jew and the Flying Dutchman?"

Billy had heard of them, but only just. He couldn't remember the stories. He gave Soobie a questioning look.

"They were condemned to live forever," said Soobie. "They found no joy in it."

The doorbell rang. Billy clasped Poopie and Soobie each in turn. He stuffed the Green Rover back in its box and as the bell rang again he hurried to the door.

"I won't tell," he called over his shoulder as he started down the stairs. "Never a word. Not if I live to be a hundred."

CHAPTER 33

The Ideal Home

"That's the one!"

Appleby was holding a glossy brochure in which there were pictures of yet another desirable residence. Tulip had seen it and discarded it. And if Granny Tulip gave the thumbs down, that was that.

Pilbeam looked up from the book she was reading. She glanced at the brochure, a luxurious booklet with the name of the house written in a lozenge cut into the glossy front cover. *The Manse*. No street number. Just a name.

"What do *you* think of it, Granny?" she said.

Tulip barely raised her eyes from her knitting.

"No use to us," she said. "No use at all."

"Why not?" said Appleby. "I know it's not quite as big as Brocklehurst Grove, but it *is* detached and well-placed. And it has a granny flat."

That was the sticking point. Tulip put down her knitting and gave Appleby one of her fiercest looks.

"If you think, for one moment, that you are going to shunt your grandfather and me off into a little granny flat tagged onto the side of the house, you are greatly mistaken. I am the mistress of the house. I always have been and I always will be. Sir Magnus is the head of the household. We are managing quite well here for the present, much better than I ever expected. We will not be rushed into just anything."

"The granny flat wouldn't be for you, grandmother," said Appleby, seeming surprised that anyone should have thought of such a thing. "It must be obvious who the granny flat would be for. 'Granny flat' is just estate agents' jargon. It doesn't mean that the person living in it has to be a granny!"

Vinetta was immediately alert.

"No, Appleby," she said. "Don't even think of it! There is no way I would allow you to have a separate entrance that you could come and go from without my knowing, not even if you share with Pilbeam."

"Don't you trust me?" said Appleby, bristling.

"No, I don't!" said her mother. "I love you and I respect all of your many talents, but I don't trust you. How could I?"

It was not necessary for Vinetta to say any more. Appleby had the sense to draw back from an argument she was bound to lose. Besides, Vinetta had got it wrong.

"You've got it wrong as usual," said Appleby in her most haughty voice. "I don't want the granny flat. I want the bedroom that looks out over the valley, the one they say has 'a breathtaking panoramic view'. There's one obvious tenant for the granny flat and I'm surprised you haven't thought of it yourself."

"Well, who?" said Vinetta, growing impatient.

"Miss Quigley, of course, who else?"

Miss Quigley glanced up quickly and then felt embarrassed when she realised that everyone in the room was looking her way.

"Me?" she said weakly.

"Yes," said Appleby. "You."

That set them all to reading the particulars of this house they had previously rejected.

"You would like it," said Vinetta, passing the brochure to Hortensia. "I'm sure you would."

Hortensia took this in slowly. She looked down at the picture on the front of the brochure, the big house with the little house tucked up cosily beside it.

"I would not be far away," she said, ". . . but I would have my very own front door."

She thought further.

"I could even have a doorbell . . .

"Any of you could come and ring it and be my visitors . . ."

Wimpey was entranced by this idea.

"I've never visited anyone before," she said. "I could bring you some flowers from the garden."

Miss Quigley smiled down at her.

"I could give you pretend tea in a willow-patterned cup," she said, ". . . and pink-iced biscuits."

One thought led to another. To have visitors would be fun; to have a private life, such as she had never really had before, would be joyful beyond words.

Her thoughts roamed on. She would be able to paint again. The little kitchen could be a studio, a sink for cleaning brushes, a bench to hold an easel . . .

Tulip took the brochure from her hands and began to peruse it more thoroughly.

The main house had three large rooms on the ground floor and four on the floor above. In the roof space was an attic with a dormer window. A single storey extension at the back was described as a conservatory.

"The conservatory is a good size," she said. "I could use that as an office, I suppose."

The 'conservatory' was a rectangular garden room stretching the full width of the house. The view from it would be of a back garden bounded by a wall or a hedge, beyond which was the graveyard of the church on the top of the hill, a church so high that its spire could be seen by sailors miles out at sea.

"It looks to be a quiet neighbourhood," said Tulip, studying carefully the outdoor shots of the building.

Consulting the A-Z map book which they always had handy when househunting, Appleby noted the cemetery and suppressed a giggle.

"Quiet as the grave," she said, all innocently.

Tulip scowled at her and added, "At least we would not be overlooked."

She turned her attention to the description of the rest of the house.

"If I have the conservatory, that will leave a good room downstairs for a bedroom," she said, turning to Joshua and deliberately ignoring her granddaughter, "Soobie's, I think. Two living-rooms, we couldn't manage with less. Look how cramped we are here! Front bedroom for Granpa and me, the other one for her ladyship, I suppose, or we'd never hear the end of it. She'll share with Pilbeam. Back bedroom for you and Vinetta. The other one would be for Wimpey."

"What about me?" said Poopie. "You've missed me out."

"You could have the attic," said Tulip. "It's big enough. What's more, it has a proper window and they say it is already in use as a bedroom."

Joshua looked at the photographs and studied the details.

"That attic'll double as a playroom," he said to Poopie. You'll have plenty of space for a train set up there."

Only Vinetta was concerned with the practicalities.

"Can we afford a house like that?" she asked Tulip.

"It will swallow most of our capital," said Tulip, "but anything smaller would be totally inadequate."

"How will we go about buying it?" said Vinetta, turning her attention to a different set of problems. "It's not as simple as popping down the Market for a bobbin of thread."

"No," said Tulip. "Simple it is not. But I have taken care of every stage in the transaction. I have the instructions all written down for Mr Dobb."

When Magnus was told about it, he scanned the brochure thoroughly, lay back on his pillows, and said, "Hmmph."

"And it's a listed building," said Tulip. "That means nobody will be able to pull it down – not for a motorway nor anything."

"Hmmph," said Magnus again.

Then, after a suitable time lapse, he added, "That alcove in the master bedroom could take quite a few shelves. Joshua can fix them up."

CHAPTER 34

Trusting Mr Dobb

Next morning, Tulip put on her coat with the fur collar and her hat with the spotted veil and went out to the telephone box. It was the beginning of October. The day was bright but chilly. So the muffled-up lady in the old-fashioned clothes did not look unduly overdressed. It was a Tuesday afternoon and North Shore Road was, in any case, nearly deserted. In the shop below the flat, Daisy was carefully unpacking a collection of alabaster statuettes.

From the living room window, the children watched their grandmother cross the road, every single one of them filled with admiration. Champions come in all shapes and sizes!

"Stay behind the curtains," Vinetta warned them. Number 39 North Shore Road had no nets at the window. Hiding was less easy than it had been at their old home.

"Mr Dobb," said Tulip, when the operator connected them, "you will remember that I asked you to undertake some additional work on our behalf?"

"Yes," said Mr Dobb cautiously. "I do remember. You did not specify exactly what it would involve. We do have our limitations, but I hope we can be of service. What is it you would like me to do for you?"

Tulip explained, in detail. Make the offer, instruct the surveyor, draw up the contract, complete the sale. And do all of this without involving his client directly in any way.

"Most of our business can be done by post. But any documents you might think too important to trust to the postal service can be sent special delivery and will be returned in the same way," said Tulip. "It suits me to conduct the whole business without personal contact. Eccentric perhaps, but I am perfectly willing to pay for my eccentricity."

What Tulip knew, absolutely, was that Mr Dobb would never suspect his long-term client of anything else. Good payers are allowed to be eccentric. If she had said to him, "I can't do all of these transactions myself because I am a rag doll" – what would he have done? *What* would he have done? Laughed at the joke, and treasured the memory!

"I will let you have my full instructions in writing," said Tulip, "and I look forward to hearing from you. Just one more thing – on no account are you to give anyone my present address. It is not my home. It is, if you like, a half-way house, a very temporary abode. I am not in the least enjoying it and I shall be very happy when I can leave. So do not fix this address on to me like a label."

Mr Dobb smiled indulgently down the phone.

"Your secret is safe with me, Lady Mennym. Not even my colleagues in this office will be permitted to share it."

That was just the first step on the way. Once the house was bought, someone else would be instructed to decorate and furnish it. And Mr Dobb would be the go-between.

"I shall give you full and very precise details of our requirements, and our spending limits. However odd this may all sound, Mr Dobb, you must remember that I always know what I am doing. This whole enterprise depends upon my giving exact instructions and your carrying them out to the letter. Past experience has taught me that I could search the whole world over and find no one more capable, more honest or more reliable than your good self!"

Mr Dobb glowed at her praise, and thought it no more than he deserved. Some of the duties she was placing upon him were outside his usual sphere of activity, but he knew the right people. He was confident of being able to get everything done.

"I will charge for my own work at an hourly rate," he said, "but in the matter of appointing people to decorate and furnish the property, my charge will not amount to much. A few phone calls should be sufficient, requesting estimates, which I will naturally pass on to you for your approval."

He paused before adding, "I'm quite looking forward to it. It will make a change from wills and probate."

Tulip's letter would be several pages long. And it would be the first of many. There would be lists and invoices and all sorts of safeguards. But the most important safeguard was Mr Dobb himself. Lady Mennym really did trust him completely.

She was wrong about thinking this service not unprecedented. No one ever had asked Mr Dobb to be such a general factotum before, but he was a man, not a little law machine, a lovely man who had old-fashioned ideals embracing loyalty, courtesy and friendship.

"And after it is all done and dusted," said Tulip to her family when she returned from the phone box, "we'll certainly not be rich any more. Though I have every hope that that will not be a permanent condition. What has been done before can be done again – eventually."

She was already knitting beautiful garments in preparation for the time when they could be sold to Harrods and even to Bloomingdales. She kept them in the bottom drawer of the chest in her bedroom knowing that Daisy would never look there. That was something they had come to understand. It had taken some of the pressure off the space beneath the wardrobe! To hide anything, all they had to do was put it out of sight.

CHAPTER 35

The House on the Hill

The house was on the other side of the River Dean, in the neighbouring town of Rimstead. It looked out over the winding river from such a height and distance that on sunny mornings it was even possible to see the sea, a shimmer of silver bordering the horizon. In the space between, the townships of Rimstead and Castledean were spread out like a map.

By night, the map disappeared. The area immediately in front of the house was in darkness, street lamps muffled by trees. In the far distance, beyond the towns in the river valley, the outlines of hills merged with the black sky. But in the centre of this picture a myriad of lights stippled the hidden landscape, shining like jewels on velvet.

That is what Soobie saw as he sat on the low stone wall of the house the Mennyms were about to buy. He had jogged across the river and up the hill, a seven mile run, and now he was taking a rest before running all the way back to North Shore Road.

To visit the house so late at night was quixotic, a mission without a purpose. He could see very little. The place was in total darkness and above the wall where he was sitting grew a very high, tangled hedge. To his left, the road in front of him plunged down into the valley. To his right, it wound on, up the hill, curving out of sight.

On the gatepost, hewn into the stone, he read the name of the house, a name half-obliterated by time. *The Manse*. The home, in days gone by, of the minister, soon to be the home of the Mennyms.

Soobie looked up at the 'For Sale' board that stood just inside the garden gate and felt momentarily nervous in case anyone else should see it and buy the house from under their noses. This house was right for the Mennyms. Without even seeing it properly, he knew how right it was.

He set off for Castledean. On the way down he didn't pass a single soul. One or two nocturnal cars went by. That was all. Then, as he came near to the Dean Bridge, he was surprised to see a figure coming towards him, a hooded figure with a familiar gait.

"Dad!" said Soobie as they drew near enough for him to be sure. "What are you doing here?"

"Just going for a walk," said Joshua. "Thought I might walk up the hill and see the house."

"I've just come from there," said Soobie. "It's too far for you to go tonight, Dad. Why not just turn round and walk home with me?"

They walked across the bridge in silence, each puzzling over the same problem.

"Has Granny thought how we are all going to get there?" said Soobie at length. "I mean – you and I could manage – but it won't be easy for the others."

"I know," said Joshua. "But your grandmother must have thought it all out. After all, she has thought of everything else."

"But what if she hasn't?" asked Soobie. "What if that's the one thing that's slipped her mind?"

*　　*　　*

When they reached the door of Number 39, Joshua let them in with the key, but Vinetta and Tulip were still up, waiting for them to return.

"Where have you been till this time?" said Vinetta, glancing up at the clock.

"Across to Rimstead," said Soobie. "I saw the house that we are going to buy. Though I could see precious little of it in the dark."

"But what did it look like?" said Vinetta. "You must have seen *something* no matter how dark it was. There would be street lamps."

"The streetlighting is poor there," said Soobie. "It's not the town centre, you know. I saw just enough to know that the garden was overgrown and on a fairly steep slope with little paved steps leading up to the door."

"Do you like it?" said Tulip.

Soobie could have made some sort of non-committal answer, but he *knew* that he liked it, and he saw no reason to hold back.

"I liked it," he said. "I liked the view of the lights all over the town, shining in the darkness. I liked the feel of the place. It felt safe."

"There is just one thing," said Joshua slowly. "It is quite a long way from here. I didn't get that far, but Soobie tells me it's at least seven miles — most of it uphill."

Vinetta looked worried. Tulip was annoyed. It *had* slipped her mind. How it could have done, she did not know. And like Appleby, she fought shy of admitting her mistake.

"When the time comes," she said huffily, "we shall all manage to get there. That is not something we need think of just now. The surveyor's report arrived in the post yesterday. I haven't had time to read it properly yet, though it seems quite satisfactory."

"I think we should all go to bed now," said Vinetta. "Just look at the time — two o'clock in the morning!"

When Tulip went into the room upstairs, Magnus was already fast asleep, spreadeagled all over the bed, purple foot trailing the floor. His wife shook his arm and said in a voice that was quiet, but urgent, "Wake up, Magnus, wake up."

Magnus came awake angrily and said, "I was *not* snoring. I never snore."

It was true, of course. He never did snore; rag dolls don't. It was simply part of an old pretend.

"That's not what I want to talk to you about," said Tulip, still in a voice not much above a whisper. "Be quiet. We don't want the others to hear. It would only worry them."

Magnus was fully awake now.

"Well?" he said grouchily. "This had better be good. You have interrupted a very serious train of thought."

"It will only be a matter of time before the house in Rimstead is ours," Tulip began, ignoring his tetchiness. "All of the wheels are in motion."

"Good," said Magnus. "And so?"

"There is a problem to which I have not given due attention," said Tulip in a peevish voice, "and neither has anybody else. I don't know why it is that I have to think of everything."

"And what might this problem be?" said Magnus. It crossed his mind that they could be running out of money. But no . . .

"The house is more than seven miles away," said Tulip. "Up a very steep hill."

"Well, so what?" said Magnus. Tulip looked annoyed. She was going to have to spell it out to him, and he must surely know 'what'!

"We'll never make it," she said, slumping down into the easy chair. "We'll never get there."

"Of course we will, woman," said Magnus. "What do you think taxis are for?"

CHAPTER 36

December

The doorbell rang loudly three times as a warning to the Mennyms that this was a different sort of Wednesday visit. It was the tenth of December – in two weeks' time it would be Christmas. Daisy had decided that the family should have a tree with all the trimmings.

Michael, who was there to carry everything, grinned as the two of them stood in the little square passage at the foot of the stairs and Daisy shouted up, "It's just me and a friend who's come to help. We have a nice surprise for you."

"You're a real turn, Daisy," said Michael, "when you've a mind to be!"

"It's a game," said Daisy, smiling at him through the branches of the Christmas tree. "Like any other game, it's only fun if you stick by the rules. I pretend they can hear me, and shouting up to tell them we're here is part and parcel of it."

Michael smiled back, but it wasn't a mocking smile. He was a nice young man, who enjoyed watching Castledean United playing football on Saturdays and who knew all about playing by the rules.

"I'll carry the tree upstairs," he said. "You can follow and show me where to put it. Then I'll come down for the rest of the stuff."

The tree was placed in the corner by the television set. It was nearly two metres high from the base of its tub to its topmost branch.

When Michael went downstairs again to fetch up the toys and the tinsel, Daisy turned to the Mennyms and said quietly, "It's a real tree, you know, not an artificial one. But you needn't worry about the needles. The shop said it had been treated in some way to stop them falling."

Michael handed in the boxes and said, "Do you want me to help to trim it?"

"No," said Daisy. "No thank you, Michael. You've done all you need to do and I'm grateful. But I'll have a good time trimming it myself. Part of the game! You can go along now. I'll see you tomorrow morning."

After Michael left, Daisy was ready for the real afternoon to begin.

Top down may be the usual way of doing things, but Daisy trimmed the tree from the bottom up. She placed big, bright baubles on the lower branches and encircled them with golden tinsel. Reaching higher, her short arms stretching as far as they could, she draped the middle of the tree with a chain of silver bells. Then she could reach no further.

"I'll just borrow this footstool," she said, taking it carefully from under Joshua's feet. She had put it there months ago, after it had been brought from the attic at Brocklehurst Grove. Now she intended to stand on it. The tree was nearly two metres in height. Daisy wasn't.

With one hand on the wall to steady herself, she stood on the footstool to put bright little apples and acorns on the higher branches.

"That looks pretty, doesn't it?" she said as she stepped awkwardly off the stool, using the top of the television set for support. "Now there's just one more thing to add."

From the smallest box she took out a little doll dressed in

silver, with a tinsel crown on its head, a wand in its hand and diaphanous wings on its shoulders. Then she stepped up onto the stool again.

The stool creaked. The Mennyms, watching her, trembled for her safety.

"Some people prefer a star on top of the tree, for the Star of Bethlehem," said Daisy as she stretched up to the topmost branch. "We always had a fairy. Leastways people call it a fairy. It's really an angel, standing there to . . ."

Then all of a sudden one little leg on the stool gave way and Daisy fell backwards towards the chair on which Joshua sat. In an instant, pact suspended, he jumped up and held out his arms to save her. She was heavy, heavier than he could manage. He staggered backwards. Pilbeam sprang up to help. Between them, they set her on her feet and held her by the shoulders till she was steady. Then, quick as a dart, they sat on their chairs again and froze.

Daisy moaned. The fall had twisted a muscle. She put one hand on her right hip and she bit her lip to ride the pain. It hurt. It hurt so much that it made her feel sick. It took all her strength of will to master it. Then, only then, she looked the dolls full in the face.

"Someone helped me there," she said. "Someone saved me."

The Mennyms remained totally impassive, each knowing that this was what the occasion demanded. Daisy took a deep breath, looked away from them and went on with the game. The pact held.

"Must have been my guardian angel," she said with a shaky laugh. "I remember at Glenthorn Drive once, it was just about this time of year . . ."

The Mennyms did not hear what she said next. She hobbled out of the living room and they heard her go into the kitchen and turn on the tap. When she returned she had a glass of water in one hand and with the other she was leaning heavily on her stick.

". . . and when all came to all," she said, "it was only the cat."

She sat down at the dining table, sipped the water, and after a few minutes was ready to finish the job she had started. The footstool was no use. One leg was buckled under it.

"I'll get Ted to mend that," she said as she put it into the corner near the sideboard. Then she went to the kitchen and brought out a strong little step-stool, the sort that doubles as a two-rung ladder.

"That's what I should have used in the first place," she said, looking towards Vinetta. "Lazy Daisy! I just couldn't be bothered to fetch it. More haste, less speed!"

She picked up the fairy from the floor, straightened its wand and its wings, and fixed it firmly on top of the tree. It was an effort. After she had finished, she switched on the television and went back to her seat by the table.

The programme was soothing, all green grass and blue sky. A man was taking a horse-drawn gipsy caravan along the highways and byways of Ireland. Some days it rained, but even the rain was sweet. Villages hid in the landscape and were vastly outnumbered by fields. The caravan moved at a snail's pace. With a world so wide, and a sky so high, why worry?

That would suit me, thought Soobie, an old yearning stirring in his heart. But blue rag dolls don't wander the earth, with or without a caravan!

"Time I was going now," said Daisy as the programme ended. "My taxi will be here any minute."

As soon as the door shut behind Daisy, Poopie came bounding down the stairs into the living room, overcome with curiosity. He knew that something had been happening.

He had heard Michael's voice and other noises. He had sat on the floor in his room keeping as still as the rabbit and the robot. Poopie had a great respect for rules. He would not be caught breaking that particular one again But, oh, it was difficult to sit there waiting for Daisy to leave!

"It's a Christmas tree!" he shouted as soon as he came into the living room. "So that's what it was all about!"

"Daisy wants us to have a proper Christmas like everybody else," said his mother.

"She nearly fell," said Wimpey to her twin. "The stool gave way and Dad and Pilbeam saved her."

"And she is still pretending that she doesn't really know that we're alive!" said Appleby. "She's incredible. I mean, just when you think the game's over, she gets up and starts again."

But Poopie wasn't concerned about these niceties. A far more interesting idea occurred to him.

"She'll probably buy us all presents," he said. "I wonder what she'll get for me?"

Granny Tulip appeared in the doorway. She had made her way more sedately down the stairs.

"We won't be here to find out," she said, choosing this moment to make public the good news.

The others all turned and stared at her.

"What do you mean, Granny?" said Pilbeam. "It's only two weeks to go."

"The keys were delivered this morning," said Tulip with great satisfaction. "The house on the hill is ours. It is ready for us to move into, completely ready. The rooms are all furnished and newly decorated, the mains are connected, so is the telephone, and, even more important, all the bills are paid."

"So when do we move?" said Vinetta. "And how do we move?"

CHAPTER 37

Preparations

"Soobie will have to jog there," said Tulip. "He's done it before. He can do it again."

"I can walk there," said Joshua. "No problem."

"You could," said Tulip slowly, "but I want you to travel in a taxi with me. We two will be the last to leave."

"Who will be in the first taxi?" asked Appleby, realising that a rota had been drawn up and thinking herself a clear candidate for leader of the expedition.

"I've made out a list," said Tulip, "and a complete plan of action, which we will not deviate from. I won't take all the credit – your grandfather was a great help. You and Granpa will be in the third taxi. Your mother will take Poopie and Wimpey in the first one. And Pilbeam, Miss Quigley and Googles will go in the second. They will leave at one hour intervals, starting at eight p.m. and finishing at eleven."

"Today?" said Wimpey, startled. She held her doll tightly to her and gazed at her grandmother, her blue button eyes seeming to widen with wonder.

It was Thursday. They had known for only one day that the move was imminent.

"No, dear," said Tulip smiling, "not today . . . We shall be leaving next Tuesday before Daisy comes again. In the meantime, there are a lot of things we have to do. It is important that we disappear without trace."

"Taxis are traceable," said Appleby. "The cab companies keep records you know. They'll know that they have picked up four lots of passengers at this address and taken them to Rimstead."

"No they won't," said Tulip. "For a start, we'll use four different companies. And our destination will not be Rimstead. It will be Castledean Central Station. There we will pick up other taxis at the taxi rank to take us on to our true destination. All we need now is to find the telephone numbers of four different taxi firms."

"I can do that," said Poopie excitedly. "I can watch for taxis out of the window and write their numbers down. They always have them printed somewhere. I've seen them."

"It will take patience," said Tulip. "Most of the taxis that pass this way will belong to the same firm. It could take you hours."

"I have more patience than anybody here," said Poopie proudly. They all remembered his marathon games with Action Men, Lego and Meccano. There was no disputing it! Poopie had patience.

So he went immediately and sat on the broad window ledge with the heavy green curtain wrapped round him and under him to shield him from the street. He was in his element sitting there, a notebook on his knee, a pencil in his hand, ready to jot down numbers, just like a train-spotter by a railway track.

"Why have I to be the one to go with Granpa?" said Appleby petulantly. "Why don't you go with him yourself? He's your husband. He should be your responsibility."

Tulip's reply was surprisingly mild and persuasive. When

it came to getting things done, Tulip could be very pragmatic in her attitude to rudeness.

"Granpa will be the most difficult to manage," she said, fixing Appleby with a glassy gaze. "You are the best one for the job. I am not tall enough to support him."

"What about Dad?" said Appleby. "What about Pilbeam?"

"Neither would be as good as you," said Tulip firmly. "You have mingled with human beings far more than the rest of us and have never been found out. You will talk to the taxi driver in your usual gabby way and distract his attention as your father and I bundle Granpa into the back seat."

Appleby opened her lips to object, but Tulip waved away the objection.

"Are you trying to tell me you won't manage it?"

"No," said Appleby, but still with a flounce in her voice. "I suppose not. If you can get him reasonably dressed, I'll manage it. But if he comes out looking like something from a pantomime, I won't make any promises."

"Your grandfather has never been other than suitably dressed for any occasion," said Tulip haughtily. "I have already bought him a coat and a hat from a catalogue."

"Yes?" said Appleby, remembering all of her grandfather's old outfits, now lost but never to be forgotten.

"Nothing fancy," said Tulip. "A full-length sheepskin overcoat and a sort of tweedy pork-pie hat with a very broad pull-down brim. And he will have boots fastened up to mid-calf."

"He'll look weird," said Appleby as she thought of how bulky he would be.

"He'll pass," said Tulip drily. "That's all you need to worry about."

In nearly three days of watching, Poopie found seven telephone numbers.

One of the telephone numbers was rejected at once because it was the taxi in which Daisy always came to work. Another was rejected because it was seen to be too familiar, the same car passing and repassing two or three times a day. But five, Tulip thought, was quite enough. It even gave a spare for emergencies!

CHAPTER 38

The Letter

"If God asked me to make my own heaven," said Hortensia, "it would be no different from this!"

She was gazing at the ground plan that the surveyor had supplied. The little boxes that marked out her territory filled her with delight.

It was Sunday morning. The whole family, with the exception of Sir Magnus of course, were sitting together in the living room. The sole topic of conversation was the coming move. Tulip looked scornfully at Vinetta over the top of Miss Quigley's head.

"She's off again, sweetness and light," she said under her breath. As always, she found the nanny irritatingly simple.

Vinetta, annoyed that her friend was being mocked, gave her mother-in-law a disapproving look and changed the subject.

"I've been thinking about Daisy," she said. "She has been very good to us. I think we should tell her that we're leaving. It doesn't seem right just to go without saying anything. It would be ungrateful."

"Rubbish," said Tulip tartly. "We can't disappear without trace if we deliberately leave traces behind us, Vinetta. Use your common sense. I agree that Daisy has been our benefactor but she's a wise enough woman to know what we've done and why. Remember the pact."

On rare occasions Vinetta could be stubborn.

"I still think we should leave her a letter," she said. "Just a word of thanks – not a forwarding address!"

There was about to be an argument when Vinetta received support from an unexpected source, for a more convincing reason.

"We do not know how we came to be in Daisy's possession," said Soobie thoughtfully. "We do not fully know the connection between Albert Pond's family and Daisy. Were we bought? Are we held in trust? Will our disappearance cause trouble for this woman who has become a dear friend to us? It matters. A letter could help in any explanations she might need to make."

"What would we write?" said Tulip. "It would have to serve the purpose well or it wouldn't be worth the effort. It is much more hazardous than doing nothing, to my way of thinking. Least said, as your Granpa would say, soonest mended."

"Doing nothing might be dangerous," said Joshua, and then Tulip realised that she was outnumbered. Joshua was still uneasy about the fact that he had left his job at Sydenham's without giving due notice. He was still afraid that some day that little bit of the past might catch up on him. It made him wary of leaving any other business unfinished!

They all pondered what was best to be done. Then Pilbeam came up with the answer.

"It will have to be the same as last time," she said. "I wrote the letter for the Gladstones to read when we went to the Doll Room. Soobie wrote the inscription on the envelope. Mother told us what to write. Remember?"

Appleby, of course, did not remember. She had had no part in that affair. It belonged to the time when the family had faced up to the possibility of death, without being totally sure that it would really happen. Appleby looked at them all and waited for a further explanation.

"I forget my exact words," said Vinetta, "but it was a letter supposed to have been written by Kate Penshaw in which she asked the new owners of her house to take care of her people. To love them, yes, to love them."

A silence came over the Mennyms as they remembered that terrible time. They took in the reality of the room where they sat. Outside, the sun was shining, a winter sun shafting the sky. Vinetta coughed before she spoke again, a nice pretend to call her listeners to attention, to nip the memory in its bud.

"And the envelope was meant to have been written forty-seven years later," she went on, "by a member of the 'Mennym' family, before they left Brocklehurst Grove, passing the plea for love onto the Gladstones."

"So," said Soobie, "if the letter is to be meaningful and effective, we must repeat the same formula. That way Daisy, and anyone else who's interested, will recognise its authenticity."

"I'll write it," said Appleby. Writing letters was one of her many talents, one she had used – and misused – for years.

"Not this time," said her mother. "This time the writing has to be Pilbeam's. And the words will again be mine."

Writing materials were taken from the sideboard drawer and Pilbeam sat down at the table ready to write.

"We'll keep it short and simple," said Vinetta. "Write this – *Dear Daisy, Thank you for helping us when our need was greatest.*"

She paused to give Pilbeam time to write. Then continued, "*Thank you for the pact. And, above all, bless you for loving Kate's People.*"

"How shall I sign it?" said Pilbeam.

"Don't," said Vinetta. "All she needs to know is in the text."

The envelope came next. Soobie used the biggest one he could find — one of a batch that Appleby had bought for Sir Magnus in the hopes that he might rouse himself and send off some manuscript or other. In a large, clear hand he wrote

---

FOR DAISY

A MESSAGE THAT WILL BE READ AFTER OUR DEPARTURE.
We are safe and need not be sought.

"That is the best I can do," said Vinetta and she slid the sheet of paper into the envelope. "I wish we could do more, but Daisy will understand why we can't."

"Where will we leave it?" asked Joshua.

"You will be the last to leave, Josh," said Vinetta, recalling Tulip's rota. "You must prop it up on the third or fourth step on the staircase so that she will see it as soon as she comes in the front door. I don't want her to come upstairs and discover our absence without due warning."

She looked wistful, then added, "It's the least, the very least, we can do."

CHAPTER 39

Packing

"I'm not going," said Poopie vehemently. "If I can't take the Lego and the Meccano and the Action Men, I'm staying here."

"Some things can go," said Tulip, "important things, but we are limited to the three hold-alls your mother bought at the Market. That will be one for each taxi except Granpa's. We obviously can't take too much. If Daisy paid for stuff from Brocklehurst Grove, and I think she probably did, it would almost seem like stealing."

"Stealing?" said Appleby. "How can we be stealing when the things were ours in the first place? I think we should order a furniture van and take the lot."

Tulip gave her granddaughter a withering look.

"Apart from the practicalities of such a ridiculous suggestion, we wouldn't need the furniture even if we could take it. Our new home is already furnished. In the main we shall take only the clothes we are wearing and anything we have bought ourselves in the past few months."

"And my Lego. And my Meccano. And my Action Men," said Poopie slowly and stubbornly.

It looked like being a fight to the death till Vinetta intervened.

"I think it's fair that you should take some toys, Poopie, but not all of them. Leave some for Billy. He is your friend, remember."

"And I'll never get to see him or talk to him again," said Poopie, thinking of another reason for not leaving.

Soobie shook his head.

"It was impossible anyway," he said. "You knew that, Poopie. You knew it from the start."

"But he can have some of your toys as a present," said Vinetta. "That's something you can do for him."

"He can have the robot," said Poopie sullenly. "It's got his batteries in it. And it was him first called it Chang."

"You'll have to leave him more than that," said Granny firmly. "Choose sensibly or you'll take nothing."

Grudgingly, Poopie agreed. So the hold-all in the first taxi was to take something from Poopie's toy cupboard.

"A whole set of something," he said. "Not much use leaving part of a set behind."

Choosing was difficult. The Lego was wonderful, the Meccano was marvellous . . . but the Action Men won the day. To Poopie they were people. He might have left the nameless warriors behind. He might even have parted with the heroic Hector. It was baleful Basil that turned the scale completely. Basil was the villain, the leader of the enemy forces, but he had lost an arm along the way. Someone less involved in his career might decide to throw him out.

"The Action Men," said Poopie. "I'll take them and their equipment. And Paddy Black will have to come. He's not a toy. He's my pretend. He's my pet rabbit."

Vinetta gave Poopie the nod to say no more. There was no point in provoking another argument with Granny Tulip.

Wimpey was much easier to deal with. Daisy had kept all of the boys' toys, meaning to please young Billy. She had sold on all of the girls' toys except the American doll that had been found with Wimpey in the Doll Room. It was a shop doll that spoke with a transatlantic accent and claimed to be called Polly whenever a loop on its back was pulled out. Wimpey loved it. Its battery had been replaced many times and it was no longer wearing its original dress, but it was still the same doll that had been bought for her at Christmas seven years ago.

"Can I take Polly?" Wimpey asked quietly, and Vinetta hugged her because she was so sweet.

At this point, Appleby, surprisingly, was not difficult at all, rather the reverse. She changed her tune completely, but still managed to sound cheeky.

"I'm not taking anything from here," she said. "When I move, I want everything new, new clothes, new music centre, new video-player, the lot. If you can afford to buy a house like that, there should be enough left over for a real new life."

"We'll see," said Tulip tersely. There was no point in arguing about future expenditure at this stage. And the less the others took with them, the more room there would be in the hold-alls for the garments she had been knitting and the wool she had not used yet.

"I wonder what Daisy will think when she finds we've gone?" said Vinetta as she packed the hold-alls. Soobie was helping, holding each bag wide open and then zipping it up when it was full. All of the stuff to be taken was arranged in neat piles on the dining table.

"We can't worry about that now," said Soobie. "We've done all we can. Unless you'd like to stay here . . .?" And the answer to that question was quite obviously no!

"I hope Kate approves," said Vinetta a little while later as she was pressing Tulip's garments down into the hold-all, cramming an extraordinary amount into a comparatively small space.

Soobie was caught off guard. He was visited by the memory of a broken door, the bricks and plaster where a doorway should have been. Words he did not mean to speak sprang to his lips.

"Of course she approves," he said tersely. "*We* approve. And we *are* Kate Penshaw, all that remains of her. She has given the whole of herself to us."

A chill came over the room.

Everyone fell silent.

Soobie's words had shocked them to the core. This was worse, much worse, than all he had ever said about the cupboard in Brocklehurst Grove not being Trevethick Street! This was as near as a rag doll could come to blasphemy.

For some minutes, nobody spoke. Nobody moved. And Soobie was filled with remorse. Granpa had once said that Appleby did not know the rules. There *are* rules, hidden rules, and no one really knows all of them! To know a rule only after you've broken it hardly seems fair . . .

Vinetta understood.

She thrust the last item into the final hold-all and began vigorously to fasten the zip. Soobie bent over to help, to hold the bulging pack together, and he was glad to have a good excuse to hide his face.

"Well, that's that job finished," said his mother in a tinny voice that made it sound as if some damage had been done to the little box inside her throat. "Now we are ready for the off."

CHAPTER 40

Taxis

By closing time on Tuesday, everything was ready. The Mennyms had stashed the hold-alls in the cupboard out of sight, just in case Daisy should have some reason to pay an unexpected visit. It was unlikely, but nothing is impossible. Precautions had to be taken.

The shutters were put in place on the windows below, more noisily than ever it seemed, but that was because all of the Mennyms were breathlessly alert. It was the eleventh hour, the time when things can go terribly wrong. But nothing did.

As soon as Daisy departed, Joshua was sent out to the phone box to book the taxis. It was incredibly smooth and easy.

Soobie set off on his run at half-past seven. The evening was cold but dry.

At eight o'clock precisely, Nolly's Cars came and picked up Vinetta and the younger twins. The driver grinned as he noticed that the children were wearing plastic animal masks. Poopie got in first, holding Paddy Black on his knee. Then Vinetta got in with the hold-all, a long nylon barrel stretched to its limit.

"I think you'd better put Polly on the back ledge," said

Vinetta to Wimpey. "Then we can hold the bag on both our knees."

Wimpey did as she was told and settled back to enjoy the ride.

At ten past nine, only ten minutes late, a car from Castledean Taxis arrived at the door of Number 39 where Miss Quigley was huddled in the doorway holding Googles wrapped up in her shawl. Pilbeam followed her into the taxi, taking hold-all number two which was full of knitting needles and wool piled on top of the book Sir Magnus had been reading.

At ten to ten, a Conroy's Mini-Hire cab turned up, stopped just under the streetlamp, and sounded its horn.

"He's early," said Magnus crossly, though he was standing in the passage all ready to go and shouldn't have been annoyed at all. When Appleby opened the door, Magnus peered along at the driver and said crustily, "It's not a he, it's a she. Might have known. Women are always the same. They can be early or late. They don't know how to be just on time."

Appleby stepped out of the doorway ahead of him and waved to the cab to come closer. Tulip and Joshua followed, supporting Magnus on either side whilst he held his cane high in his hand.

The driver backed up slowly to the curb near the door and was about to get out and help.

"It's all right," said Appleby. "Stay where you are. For goodness' sake don't try to help him. He's completely doolally. I'm in charge of him. You'll be safe enough. He's quite harmless really, but he can't stand strangers coming anywhere near him. It sends him off into hysterics."

The driver looked worried. The girl on the pavement, a gangly teenager in anorak and jeans, wearing absurd dark glasses that were much too big for her face, could be no older than sixteen or seventeen at the most. How would the old man, doolally or not, react to her cheek?

"It's all right," said Appleby, seeing the doubtful expression on the woman's face. "He can't hear a word I'm saying. He's stone deaf, been that way for years."

Magnus, hearing every word, was silent but furious. His wife and son pushed him into the door of the cab, like a housewife bundling laundry into a washing machine. Magnus in a sheepskin coat was very bulky, and the taxi was quite small. His pork-pie hat was well down over his brows and his turned-up collar enveloped his chin so that all that could be seen was some sign of his white moustache. The purple feet were hidden in a very large pair of leather boots.

Mission accomplished, Tulip and Joshua retreated to the doorway. Appleby got into the back seat next to Magnus whose only response to her impertinence was to spread himself out across the seat and give her as little room as possible.

"You're very young," said the driver over her shoulder. "It's a wonder they've left it up to you to be responsible for him."

"I'm a lot older than I look," said Appleby, "and I really am the best one to manage him. They all say that. He lives in a world of his own. Sometimes he thinks he's Oliver Cromwell. But he seems to know who's in charge when I'm around."

Magnus dug his left elbow into Appleby's side and kept it there. Not much of a punishment, there were no ribs to bruise, but it was the best he could do, for the moment . . .

"Central Station?" said the driver as she started up the engine. "Got far to go after that?"

"Train to London. We'll be met there by two male nurses and that'll be the end of my job. They're taking him off to a clinic in the South of France that specialises in his type of case."

"That'll cost something," said the driver.

"He can afford it. He's loaded. They're all loaded except me. I'm just a poor relation."

By now, Appleby had gone well over the top and the driver no longer believed a word she was saying. Loaded? And living in a flat in North Shore Road? She asked no more questions but just shrugged her shoulders and kept her eyes on the road. When they came to the station, Appleby gave the driver an extra large tip to demonstrate their wealth. Then she disgorged her grandfather from the back seat, set one hand on to his cane, and draped the other round her shoulders.

"Good luck, pet," called the driver, "wherever it is you're going!"

The fourth and final taxi arrived spot on eleven o'clock. Tulip, Joshua and one well padded hold-all got into the back with no trouble at all.

"Central Station," said Joshua. And not another word passed anyone's lips till the journey was over.

Only one thing went really amiss in the whole operation. A small thing. A very small thing to everyone but Wimpey. Polly, the American doll, was left on the back ledge in the taxi.

A station taxi, as big and as black as a hearse, swallowed each group of Mennyms in turn and transported them across the river and up to the church on the top of the hill. From there they walked down a short path to their new home, and into hard-won anonymity.

CHAPTER 41

Slowly, Very Slowly

On Wednesday morning, Daisy shut up shop at eleven-thirty. She had an appointment at the Infirmary. They were going to x-ray that pesky hip! Ever since she'd slipped off the stool, it had been giving her twinges and slowing her down.

"If I get any slower, I'll be going backwards," she had joked to the doctor down at the surgery. She was not too optimistic about the outcome of the hospital visit, but she was determined to conquer this new disability, even if it should prove to be permanent.

She walked along the pavement, leaning heavily on her stick, and rang the doorbell at Number 39, rang it three times to make sure the Mennyms would hear. She was earlier than usual and did not want to alarm them. This Wednesday she would not be paying them their usual afternoon visit and she wanted them to know.

She opened the door with her key, went into the passage and called up the stairs, "My taxi's coming any minute. I won't be up to see you today. I've got an appointment at the hospital. Just a check-up, you know. It's a nuisance, but it's best to be careful."

Daisy hesitated, standing there in the passage, door half-open, looking up at the narrow staircase. The way I feel today, she thought, I couldn't face those stairs even if I weren't going to the hospital.

Then she saw the letter. A very large white envelope with her own name on it was standing tilted against the rise of the fourth step.

Bending forward slowly, painfully slowly, she picked it up and went out into the daylight to look at it more closely.

The street was empty. She held the envelope up to the light and gasped as she read the inscription.

FOR DAISY

A MESSAGE THAT WILL BE READ AFTER OUR DEPARTURE.
We are safe and need not be sought.

Just then, the taxi drew into the curb in front of the shop. Daisy saw it and quickly closed the door of Number 39 behind her.

"I'm here," she called, and the driver, seeing her through his mirror, backed up to where she was standing, stick crooked over her arm, bag in one hand, letter in the other.

"They tell me it's the Infirmary today," said the driver, the same one who usually drove her home to Hartside Gardens.

"Yes," said Daisy as she settled into the back seat. "Just for a check up. Make sure the hip's all right."

She sat back, tore open the envelope and read its contents. The taxi drove up Deacon Street and past the Theatre Royal. It crossed the High Street into Albion Street and then went under the motorway and round into Dickinson Road.

"We're here," said the driver. "Which entrance is it you want?"

Daisy looked vague as if brought abruptly out of a dream.

"Entrance?" she said.

"The way in," said the driver with a laugh. "You're not up to your usual form today!"

Daisy laughed back.

"It's old age, you know. Makes the mind wander. Still, at least I still have a mind capable of wandering, which is more than can be said of me poor old pins!"

"Well, whither do we wander now?" said the driver. "There's a chap in the car behind us getting very puzzled."

"Second on the right – x-ray department," said Daisy, laughing again, "and less of your lip!"

The letter was thrust into her handbag and left for later, but its contents kept humming around in her brain like bees. The rag dolls, her family of Mennyms, were gone. The message seemed quite clear. They had left of their own accord and gone to some place of safety that they knew. Knew *now* – but not before?

That was a puzzle, a mystery. Had their bodies gone, or just their spirit? Would inanimate dolls be found in the flat above the shop? Daisy then realised that the message was not clear at all.

The x-ray took very little time and its result was instantaneous. There was no fracture, only a strained muscle which was causing some sciatica. The hip itself was holding up well.

"You're a strong woman, Daisy," said the specialist. "It's the will that does it. You'll go on forever! But I'd like you to take things a bit easier. No lifting, no straining, no climbing stairs, just plenty of rest, till this settles down again."

"If I stop, I'll seize up," said Daisy. "That's what happens to old engines!"

"I'm not asking you to stop," said the doctor with a laugh at his stubborn patient. "Just take a breather!"

But Thursday found Daisy back at work as usual. Nothing would have kept her away from the shop that day. For months she had pretended not to hear the noises in the flat above. Today she was listening for them, listening and hoping. The bell over the door jangled. Customers came and went. But from the floor above came not a sound.

One very curious thing did occur. At about two o'clock in the afternoon a taxi drew up outside the shop with 'Nolly's Cars' painted on the door panel. The driver got out, carrying something in his hand, and went to the door of Number 39. Daisy did not see him. She was busy writing.

The taxi driver rang the doorbell of the flat, then waited. He rang again and waited again. When it became clear that no one was coming to open the door, he looked around, paused to think, and then made up his mind. The shop was below the flat. Whoever was in the shop must know their upstairs neighbours.

"Hello, missus," said the driver as he came in and saw Daisy sitting at the octagonal table.

"Yes?" said Daisy, looking up from her work.

"The people in the flat upstairs . . ." he began.

Daisy started but said nothing.

The young man held up a doll. It was Polly. Daisy recognised it immediately.

". . . their little girl left this doll in the back of my cab. I thought she might like to have it back, but there's nobody home."

"That's all right," said Daisy. "I'll take care of it."

He handed the doll over. Daisy took the doll and smiled.

Then she put her hand to her bag to take out her purse.

"No," said the driver, seeing what she intended. "I don't want nothing. I've just taken a fare down to the Old George. So I was almost passing, as you might say."

"Well, thank you," said Daisy. "Thank you very much."

The driver was leaving the shop when Daisy called after him, "Where were they going when she left her doll?"

"Central Station," said the driver. "I suppose they were off to catch a train."

After he went out, the bell jangling as the door closed behind him, Daisy put the doll on the shelf by the telephone and tried to go on with her work, but thoughts got in the way. The Mennyms *had* left. They had left by taxi and the driver had thought they were human.

CHAPTER 42

Mrs Cooper

"I see you've got rid of the dolls up there," said Mrs Cooper. "Would you like me to bring the tree down? It would look nice in the shop window."

She had come into the shop to collect her wages. Friday was not just the day when she cleaned the house upstairs. It was also pay day.

Daisy was in her usual seat at the octagonal table, filing boxes in front of her, pretending to work. But she had been waiting tensely for just this moment. Till now the evidence for the disappearance of the Mennyms had been purely cirumstantial. This was the first positive confirmation that they had really departed. Someone had been upstairs, and looked around, and found an empty flat.

Mrs Cooper's blunt phrasing hurt, being so matter of fact, almost expressing approval, but Daisy knew that no harm was intended.

She looked up at her cleaning lady.

"It wouldn't be worth the trouble for the few days that are left," she said. "Michael will take it down after the holiday."

Daisy handed over Mrs Cooper's wages, complete with Christmas bonus, for which she received a brief thank you. Then there was a pause, an inexplicable hiatus.

Mrs Cooper did not turn to go. She stood her ground, silently making up her mind what to say next. She dropped her purse into her shopping bag and pulled the zip along.

"It's a nice flat, that," she said tentatively.

"Yes, it is," said Daisy, smiling. "I should know. I was born there!"

"I've always thought it was a shame to let it go to waste, especially now that it isn't really a store-room or anything else," said Mrs Cooper. "It was different when the dolls were there. It was like a sort of museum, wasn't it?"

Daisy nodded, wondering what was coming next.

"Now it's empty," said Mrs Cooper as she stood fumbling with her brown leather gloves, straightening them out before easing them onto her fingers.

Daisy thought, empty. Yes, empty. It was a sad word, sad meaning . . .

"Have you any mind to let it?" said Mrs Cooper.

"Let it?" said Daisy. "I couldn't do that. It would cost a fortune to make it fit to live in. No heating, no hot water, and the toilet's downstairs in the backyard. Nobody nowadays would put up with that."

"People modernise places," said Mrs Cooper. "It's done everywhere. I wonder you haven't thought of it before. You could get a good rent for it."

"Too much bother," said Daisy. "And over the years we have made good use of the space, you know."

"But not now," said Mrs Cooper.

Daisy was puzzled. At that moment, she would have preferred to be alone, to mourn the loss of her family in silence. Belief is such a strange commodity. Till today, she had hoped, vainly hoped, that the Mennyms were still upstairs. Now that she had undeniable proof of their departure, she wanted to think of that and that alone. Instead, here was Mrs Cooper, with unusual volubility, chuntering on about the empty flat.

"It looks lovely now it's properly furnished and all cleaned up," she said. "I was just saying to my son how nice it was. All it needs is a plumber to put in some central heating and a new bathroom."

Daisy knew that that was much more complicated and expensive than it sounded. But her mind was elsewhere and she said absently, "I suppose so."

"My son's a plumber," said Mrs Cooper in a rush. "He could modernise it for you. Him and his wife are looking for somewhere to rent. They don't want to take on a mortgage, not these days. It's too risky."

When Daisy did not reply, she went on to say, "They'd be very good tenants. It wouldn't be like letting to strangers."

"Ah!" said Daisy, calling her thoughts to attention and focussing on what Mrs Cooper was saying. The cleaning woman looked at her anxiously.

"It takes a bit of thinking about," said Daisy carefully. "It's a new idea to me. I won't say no, but I do need time to consider it."

"You can't say fairer than that," said Mrs Cooper, but looked as if she would like to say more.

Mrs Cooper 'did' Daisy's bungalow in Hartside Gardens on Mondays and Thursdays, letting herself in with the key and departing like the cobbler's elves, leaving neat evidence of her visits. Friday was usually the only time she met Daisy face to face.

"I'll be going now," she said. "I see you're busy. If you make up your mind, one way or the other, you could mebbes just leave me a note at Hartside and, if the answer's yes, I'll tell our Joseph to come to the shop and see you."

"That'll be fine," said Daisy.

"It's a shame to leave a good house empty these days," said Mrs Cooper above the jangling of the door as she opened it, "with the housing lists so long."

That was enough to influence her employer. The rent would not be a real attraction, a game not worth the candle, but Daisy would think further of a flat going to waste and a young couple glad of a home.

"I've never thought of it that way before," she murmured. Then, raising her voice, she said, "I'll shut up shop early on Monday, Mrs Cooper. If you wait till I get home, we can talk about it then."

It was four-thirty when Mrs Cooper finally closed the shop door behind her. Alone at last, Daisy neither wept nor wondered. She just sat at the octagonal table feeling as empty as the flat above. From her handbag she drew out the letter the Mennyms had left and she read it over again. A hundred readings would not suffice. It was a blank wall.

A blank wall, thought Daisy, a nothingness.

Then with alarm she thought, what on earth will I tell the Ponds? What will they think? What will they believe?

CHAPTER 43

Albert and Lorna

"That was Daisy," said Albert replacing the receiver on the telephone. "She wants to see us. She's asked us to take the letter that was left with the dolls in Brocklehurst Grove."

Lorna had just come downstairs after putting Matthew to bed. She gave her husband a look of dismay. It was the Saturday before Christmas. Her parents and the rest of the Gladstones had just moved into Number 5 Brocklehurst Grove. They had sold their old house, bought new furniture and carpets, and finally persuaded Jennifer that Number 5 was as free of memories as any house could ever be. And to that end they had agreed to stay away from the shop in North Shore Road.

"Did she say why?" asked Lorna. Then she added anxiously, "I hope she doesn't want us to take the dolls back. There's no way we could do it. And finding someone else to care for them might be . . ." she paused, ". . . would be impossible."

Lorna had championed the cause of the dolls from the beginning. She had taken seriously the plea to love them, but her mother would not hear of their remaining in the house at Brocklehurst Grove. Finding a real 'carer', willing and able to take on the task, had been difficult. So Lorna and Albert had been delighted when they discovered Daisy.

"I've said we'd go and see her on Monday morning," said Albert. "Your mother will be looking after Matthew then anyway whilst we are supposed to be finishing our Christmas shopping. We needn't tell her anything."

At eleven o'clock the following Monday, Lorna and Albert went into Daisy's shop and waited discreetly till her customer left.

"Have a nice Christmas, Mr Featherstone," said Daisy, "and a happy New Year."

As the door closed behind him, Daisy looked towards Albert and said, "Could you just put the catch on, and turn the CLOSED sign towards the street? Save my poor legs! Then let's go to the kitchen and I'll make you some tea."

'Some tea' was the usual mountain of cakes and sandwiches set out on the big square table.

"Sit down and eat up," said Daisy. "The cold will be making you hungry."

As soon as they were seated, Lorna launched straight into the reason for their visit.

"Albert says you have something to tell us?" she said abruptly, sounding almost hostile in her nervousness.

"Yes," said Daisy. "It's very difficult. I hardly know how to begin. You might decide that we should call in the police."

Her two visitors looked astounded.

"It's the rag dolls," said Daisy. "They aren't here any more."

"Stolen?" said Albert. "Have you been burgled?"

"I don't know," said Daisy. "I will tell you the facts, few as they are, and then you must judge for yourselves. All of the dolls were in the flat when I visited them a week gone Wednesday. That I do know. I didn't go up to see them last Wednesday because I had a hospital appointment. And on Friday my cleaning lady told me that the dolls had disappeared."

"But there's more to it than that?" Albert said.

Daisy nodded.

She handed them the letter the Mennyms had left behind them.

Lorna looked at it and was mystified. She took the letter she had brought with her out of her handbag and compared the two. The envelopes (in Soobie's hand) looked identical. The letters, both written by Pilbeam, were a good match.

"It's the same writing," she said. "The same printing as on the old envelope, the same script as in the old letter that the family who lived in Brocklehurst Grove left behind them."

Albert took it from her and scanned it carefully, not just for the writing but for the words and the meaning.

Dear Daisy, Thank you for helping us when our need was greatest. Thank you for the pact. And above all, bless you for loving Kate's People.

"It's not signed," said Albert, "but it is addressed to Daisy and 'Kate's People' are clearly the dolls."

"What do they mean by 'the pact'?" asked Lorna. "Whoever wrote this obviously thinks that you are going to understand it, Daisy."

Daisy quailed. How could she explain 'the pact' to these young people without explaining everything? They would never understand. What might they believe? That she was confused, weak in the head? What was it they called it nowadays?

"I don't know," Daisy lied. "Your guess is as good as mine."

It was, after all, only half a lie, for knowing and believing are not the same thing.

"Whatever this means or doesn't mean," said Albert at length, "it can only be the work of the previous tenants of Number 5. The Mennyms, for some reason known only to themselves, have taken the dolls back again. No one else could have written that letter. We always knew they were peculiar people."

Albert's mention of 'the Mennyms', the real Mennyms and not the doll family, stirred something in Daisy's consciousness. She looked down at the letters again. Then she came to the edge of the truth, a border so strange that what lay beyond was past imagining.

"What if the dolls *were* the Mennyms?" she said. "What if there were no other . . ."

She faltered, aware that she had said far more than she had meant to say.

Lorna gulped and lifted her cup to take a sip of tea. It was empty.

"Your cup's empty," said Daisy, glad to change the subject. "Let me pour you another."

Embarrassed, Lorna passed the cup to her hostess.

"Have another sandwich or some of my chocolate cake," said Daisy to Albert.

They all sat eating the cakes and sandwiches without tasting them, just automatically putting hand to mouth. The Ponds were eyeing Daisy warily. Daisy was trying hard to be natural whilst her thoughts raced off on a path of their own.

"I don't see why the previous owners didn't just come to us and ask for them. We would have handed them over," said Lorna, leaving Daisy out of the equation altogether. "It's not as if we wanted them for ourselves."

She looked helplessly at Albert.

"Do we *have* to call the police?" she said.

"I think not," said Albert. "The dolls are gone and I cannot see that we would ever get them back again. And if we do tell the police there is every possibility that your mother would get to know. She would hate it. You know she would."

That was exactly what Lorna had begun to think.

"If the Mennyms *did* find out where the dolls were and for

some eccentric reason wanted to steal them, I'm not sure that it would matter," she said. "They kept them beautifully for more than forty years. They would surely not destroy them now."

As Daisy listened, she found it hurtful that her interest in the dolls should be so completely ignored. Albert, she noted, looked rather uncomfortable.

"It must have been a shock to find them gone," he said quickly when Lorna finished speaking. "What will you do with the flat now? Do you feel lumbered with all that furniture?"

Daisy smiled at him.

"I have plans," she said. "Furniture is my business – you mustn't forget that. As for the shock, it's still sinking in. I will miss the Mennyms. They've been good company."

Albert was glad he had spoken. He knew only too well that though Lorna was really good-hearted she could be very thoughtless. Blame it on her youth! The words were unsaid, but the look told Daisy what he meant.

"I think we should be going now," said Lorna, looking at her watch. "There's such a lot to do, and my mother will be wondering where we've got to."

So the ordeal was over.

The Ponds thanked Daisy for their meal, both of them hugged her before leaving, and all of them knew that they would never meet again.

CHAPTER 44

Billy Returns

On Christmas Eve, Billy came to visit his Aunt Daisy hoping to play with the dolls again, longing to talk to Poopie. Daisy had not seen him since the summer holidays and she had not told him that the dolls were no longer there.

It was one o'clock on Wednesday afternoon. The shop was already shut. Jamie Maughan stopped the car outside the door but neither he nor Mollie got out. Just Billy.

"We'll be back just after four o'clock," said Jamie. "So tell Daisy to be ready for the off. We won't have time for tea. Make sure you tell her that."

"She'll know already," said Billy. "You've told her on the phone six or seven times over!"

"That won't stop her wanting to give us a big feed!" said his dad with a grin. "You know what she's like!"

Daisy was going to spend the Christmas holiday with the family at Bedemarsh Farm. It had all been arranged, down to Billy's own afternoon at the shop whilst his parents went off to buy a few last minute surprises.

"Come into the back, Billy," said Aunt Daisy. "I've got the kettle on and there's turkey and stuffing sandwiches and sweet mince pies."

Billy followed her through the shop into the kitchen and sat down at the table. This all seemed to him an irksome preliminary. In the months since summer the memory of his talk with the Mennyms had not blunted. It was carefully stored knowledge that made him feel marked out and special. He told no one, but the not-telling was a strain. And the only relief would be to meet the dolls again, to go into the room upstairs and play with Poopie. In speaking to Daisy, he was cautious, wondering just how much she really knew.

"I've missed the dolls," he said. "It seems ages since I saw them."

Daisy poured the tea, but said nothing. She too was wondering how much to tell. The departure of the Mennyms was full of unknowns.

"There's something I have to talk to you about," she began when she sat down beside him after refilling the kettle for the next brew. She had decided to come at the story from an angle, not to meet it head on.

Billy looked up from his tea-cup and wondered what was coming next.

"It's me Will," said Daisy. "I've been meaning to make one for ages."

Billy looked uncomfortable. He was just turned fourteen and reluctant to talk about things like wills. It was morbid.

"No," said Daisy laughing at his solemn face. "I'm not going to die yet. But I'm not getting any younger and it's sensible to be prepared. Besides, I always swore I'd see to it that Lily and Polly Waggons would be looked after."

Billy knew all about the sisters who had sat forever in the shop window. He smiled at Daisy and said, "I'll look after them if I can."

"You can," said Daisy. "If it's what you want, the shop can be yours. It needn't be your life's work You can get somebody in to run it for you if you like. But I want you to try and keep the shop going and to let my girls stay in their places in the window. Do you think you could do that?"

"I know I could," said Billy. "I could look after the dolls upstairs an' all. I would never let anyone hurt them."

Daisy was about to answer when there was a noise from the flat above, as of somebody moving furniture. A heavy weight was being dragged slowly across the floor. Billy was just about to take a bite out of his mince pie. He stopped and gasped.

"They're moving about up there," he said in a voice full of amazement. "I've never heard them moving about before!"

What he really meant was far more complex. It was clear from Daisy's lack of reaction that the noise upstairs was no surprise to her. Had she moved on? Did she know more than she'd known before?

Then, in the silence that followed, they heard laughter, a girlish giggle.

"They're laughing," said Billy, looking wonderingly at Daisy. Were the rag dolls out in the open? And Daisy was coping. Her heart had not stopped!

Daisy saw the look on his face and said quickly, "That's not them. That's Joseph and Sally, Mrs Cooper's son and his wife – you know Mrs Cooper, the woman who does my cleaning . . ."

"But . . ." began Billy, puzzled.

"They live up there now. They moved in yesterday. They've got all sorts of plans for the property, but I let them move straight in, to have a proper home for Christmas."

"What about the dolls?" said Billy. "The Mennyms? Where are they now?"

"That," said Daisy, "is something else we'll have to talk about."

Billy listened dazed as she told him the whole story, showed him the letter the Mennyms had left on the stairs, told him about the taxi driver who had returned Wimpey's doll. Daisy gave him the doll to hold in his hands as if it were evidence. Billy pulled the ring on the doll's back and heard it say in its flat little voice, "I'm-Polly. What-are-you-called? Would-you-like-a-Chocolate-Milk?"

"We should put it in the window," he said, wanting a ceremony, something to mark the departure. "Then if the little girl ever passes this way she will know where it is."

Billy knew it would be no more than a gesture. The talking doll could be put in the window. It was very improbable that the doll with the blue ribbons would ever see it, but if she did she would not come in to claim it. Billy knew that.

And so did Daisy. Nevertheless, she hobbled on her stick to the window where Polly Waggons sat and she propped up the doll beside the folds of the long grey skirt so that it faced out towards the street.

"There now," she said to the wooden betty lady who sat unmoving with her fingers spread out on the typewriter keys, "you have a little girl to sit by you. Her name's the same as yours!"

CHAPTER 45

The Last Chapter

It was half-past three.

Daisy and Billy had drunk yet another cup of tea and talked more and more about the dolls that had once lived upstairs. Billy went even further back, recalling the time he had taken make-believe meals to the blue doll in the loft at Bedemarsh Farm. He remembered the girl doll skipping on the path outside Comus House. But he made no mention of that Wednesday in August about which Soobie had warned him to be silent.

"Have another pie," said Daisy. "There's plenty left for your mam and dad. And I've got another plate of sandwiches in the fridge. Better take them out now so they won't be too cold."

"Oh!" said Billy. "I forgot. Dad says we have to be ready to go straightaway. They aren't coming in. They want to get straight home. And have you got your case packed?"

Daisy laughed.

"No need to worry," she said. "I'm all ready for my holidays! And if they really aren't coming in, I'll put the rest of the food into a carrier bag to take with us. Waste not, want not!"

As she wrapped up the sandwiches, Billy watched her

thoughtfully. Even now he did not feel free to talk about his own special encounter with the dolls.

"What do you really believe?" he said.

"About the Mennyms?" said Daisy as she continued to make neat little packages of food and put them into a Tesco bag.

"Yes," said Billy. "Do you think somebody stole them? Or do you think they really could have gone away of their own accord?"

Daisy stopped to consider. She looked at Billy across the table and weighed her words carefully before she spoke.

"What I believe needn't be true," she said. "You do know that?"

"Yes," said Billy slowly. "I think I do."

"Then, for my own part, in my own private opinion, I believe they somehow had the means and the ability to find somewhere else to live — some place where not even Daisy Maughan would visit them. I believe, if you like, that they are living happily ever after."

Billy remembered the story of the Flying Dutchman and wondered what living happily ever after might really mean.

"Some day I'll find them," he said. "Some day I'll see them again. I'll talk to them and get to know them properly."

He thought awhile and then had another wave of inspiration.

"It might be possible to trace them," he said. "To find out where they went. Taxi drivers might know. They couldn't all have gone in one taxi. Somebody at the Central Station might have noticed them, even if they were all wrapped up in hoods and things."

"No!" said Daisy sharply. "You mustn't look for them. You mustn't ever look for them. It took a tremendous effort for them to leave here. To pursue them would be cruel. Think of the stories you have read, the films you have seen. The

Mennyms have gone. For us, that is the end. We will never see them again."

Her words gave Billy pause for thought. How much did Daisy know? He would never dare to ask. He began to suspect that she knew even more than he did. Suddenly he was able to see the dolls with Daisy's eyes, to have some idea of what it all might mean. He stood up and placed one hand on her shoulder.

"You're right," he said. "I don't quite know how or why, but I believe you are right."

Daisy smiled up at him. Billy's ginger hair was less wispy, his shoulders just a little bit broader than they had been on his last visit, and he must have added an inch or two to his height.

"You do keep on growing," said Daisy, seeming to change the subject. "I wish you'd give me the recipe."

"You're not little, Aunt Daisy," said Billy, knowing perfectly well what she really meant. "In my eyes, you're as tall as a tree."

In the street outside, Jamie Maughan's car drew up in front of the shop. He looked for signs of his aunt and his son emerging and when there were none he sounded the horn twice over. It was already dark, and he was anxious to get out of the town before the rush hour. Daisy handed Billy her case, looped the Tesco bag over her arm and, leaning heavily on her stick, made for the door. Billy walked ahead of her to the car.

"I won't be a minute, Jamie," she called as she came outside. "Have a bit of patience, won't you! I'll just have to lock the front door. The lads will be around later to do the shutters."

She turned the key in the lock and then fixed a padlock in place just below it. Unhurried, she glanced at the wooden betty dolls in the window, turning her head first to one and then to the other.

"Happy Christmas, Lily," she said. "Happy Christmas, Polly."

Then she looked out into the darkness and added, "Happy Christmas, Mennyms, wherever you may be. And God bless you, Kate Penshaw."

For Daisy understood the secret of the Mennyms.